ii

Also by Tony H. Latham

Analyzing Ballistic Evidence, On-Scene by the
Investigator

Trafficking, A Memoir of an Undercover Game
Warden

Five Fingers

Seven Dead Fish

By

Tony H. Latham

Acknowledgments

Thanks to my sister, Jane Griffith and her red pen. She may have put as much blood and sweat into this story as I did.

Epigraph

"What would good do, if evil didn't exist and what would the earth look like if all the shadows disappeared?"

\- Mikhail Bulgakov

Chapter 1

Her shriek turned his gut. She was sitting in a chair; her wrists were secured to the seat's arms. Duct tape covered her mouth, and it didn't make sense. Her face was flushed, and her eyes looked like ivory colored marbles. The second scream came from within his head as he watched the revolver's hammer being drawn back. The barrel was in his mouth, and it had an odd soap-like taste. The man holding the gun had the same pupilless iced eyes. He knew what was next. But the third scream came from his phone and roused him. He realized it was *the dream*.

Glancing at the digital clock on the nightstand, he saw what he already knew, it was 3:43 a.m.

He grabbed for the glowing phone. It was sheriff Fred Mendiola. He slid his finger across the cell phone's screen and brought it to his ear. The heel of his hand felt sweat on the side of his face. "Yeah?" His voice was gravelly as if he'd been yelling.

"Hey, I need your help," Mendiola said. "Sorry about the call. I could use your expertise out here."

"What ya got?" His heart was still pounding from the dream.

"I'm not sure. I need you to come look at a boot we

found."

Charley Cove faltered, trying to make sense of what
he'd just heard but still befuddled by the dream. *A boot?*
His eyes squinted in the dark room, his mind drifting to
her marbled eyes. "Did you say, 'boot'?" He was thinking
the sheriff must have said "bullet." He moved his bare foot
over to the other side of the bed. She wasn't there.

"Yeah, we found a boot out here at this crash. Jenks got
in a pursuit, and the guy rolled. I'm hoping you can help
us out with time of death."

Cove was beginning to wake up. Nothing in the short
conversation had made any sense. If Deputy Jenks had
gotten in a pursuit, and the guy he was chasing had
crashed and been killed, why the mystery over *when* he'd
died? And why would they call out a game warden for time
of death on a human?

"Where you at?" Cove asked.

"Just past the airport on the highway, that long curve."
He paused. "You don't sound awake, Charlie. I'll call
dispatch and have a thermos ready. We could use a cup
too."

Cove silently agreed with Mendiola's assessment of his
mental acuteness–things weren't making any sense. "I'll
be there in a bit," he replied and set the phone back down.
He put his hands behind his head, hunched over and
stretched his spine. His back popped, and it seemed to
help clear the haze in his mind. Turning the nightstand
light on, he squinted and looked down at his dog. "Annie,
we gotta go to work." The chocolate lab was lying on a red
plaid dog bed. She had her ears cocked and was watching
him.

Cove gimped into the bathroom, turned on the shower and reached for an open bottle of aspirin sitting next to the sink. He shook three out, chucked them into his mouth and swallowed a half glass of water. He looked up. The man that stared back from the mirror looked as if he'd been in a foot race and had lost. His skin was sweaty; his eyes were sunken and red. His beard needed a shave.

He ran his hand through his hair, stepped into the warm water and turned the hot knob up to the point where it started to hurt. He closed his eyes and let the scalding water run over his head. He wanted to burn the dream away.

His mind went back to the call. A boot. Time of death. Jenks in a pursuit. Who'd crashed? Maybe the guy had poached a deer. That would explain why Fred had called. Perhaps figuring out when the deer had been killed would help solve something else that they were working on. But the call had seemed to focus on a boot. The more he thought about Mendiola's call, the more confused he was.

When he pulled beside the sheriff's office, a thirtyish looking slender woman stepped out from the door. She was wearing jeans, and her dark hair touched the epaulettes on her navy-blue uniform shirt. She reached through the window and handed him a large stainless thermos bottle.

"Morning, Charlie, I'm Barb, we talked on the radio the other night." She smiled, showing white teeth. "Fred said to make sure you've got your thermometer." She gave her head a curious little shake. "What's that all about?"

"I don't have a clue. What the hell happened?" he asked while unscrewing the cap from the thermos. Lifting his coffee mug up into the light from the open doorway, he started to pour.

"Jenks got in a pursuit, and he lost it."

Cove stopped pouring the coffee and looked at the dispatcher. "Is he okay?"

She nodded her backlit head. "Yeah, it was the guy he was chasing. They're flying him out to Idaho Falls. It doesn't sound good; his blood pressure was bottomed. The EMTs radioed the clinic and said they couldn't get an IV started. Made my stomach churn."

"Fred said something about a boot." He looked at her and tried to read her face in the darkness. "What's that all about?"

A phone rang from inside the building. She stepped back towards the open door. "I gotta get that."

Cove raised his voice to a half holler. "Thanks for the coffee." The green glow from the truck's dashboard highlighted his face. He took a sip of coffee and dropped the transmission into drive.

When he passed the clinic, it was lit up. An ambulance was parked at the side, and a TwinStar helicopter sat on the illuminated pad.

Five miles later, three vehicles with flashing light bars marked the scene. Two were flashing blue and one was flashing yellow. They were parked on both sides of the highway with their headlights on. Fifty yards off the pavement, a fourth set of dim headlights shined at an odd angle. The yellow flashers were coming from a wrecker. He could see the driver slumped in the truck's seat. A blue light exposed his open mouth. Cove turned around and parked behind the wrecker. He turned on his emergency flashers, left his blue overhead strobe flashing and killed his engine. As he got out, he could see the large silhouette of Fred Mendiola approaching with a flashlight beam bouncing around him as if he were looking for something.

In his own, low-key way, Mendiola had taken Charlie under his wing eight years ago. He'd mentored Cove on the craft of small-town law enforcement and tried to teach him how to survive. He'd opened his home to Cove on several occasions for home-cooked meals with his family. There had been times when the two had stood side by side with guns drawn—which created a bond that only a lawman might understand. But most importantly, Mendiola had supported him when he could have thrown him under the bus. On the other side of the coin, it was clear to Cove that Mendiola didn't hold wildlife crimes very high on the scale.

"Charlie," the sheriff yelled, "grab your thermometer, and I'll show you the boot."

Cove paused, still not understanding. He reached back into his truck and pulled a tubular stainless steel thermometer from the visor and slipped it next to the pen in his shirt pocket. He pulled his Surefire light out of a pouch from his duty belt and shined it around the edge of the road. He could see where the vehicle had skidded off the pavement, slid through the barrow pit and snapped a wooden fence post like a pencil. He shined the light around, wondering what Mendiola was looking for. The night smelled of early summer alfalfa, but there was a tinge of the fruit-like odor of antifreeze. He could see at least three large divots in the field where the vehicle had bounced, flipping end over end.

"What's going on?"

"I don't know," Mendiola answered. "Can't say for sure it's even part of this crash, but it has to be." The sheriff shined his light towards the broken fencepost. "It's right here. One of the EMTs tripped on it." He shined his light next the sheared-off fencepost and exposed a shiny plastic lump. Mendiola walked over, reached down with a nitrile-gloved hand and lifted a black garbage sack off whatever it was concealing. "I figured I should cover it."

Cove shined his light on it. They were looking down at a left-footed boot. It was a sand-colored, lace-up made from a combination of leather and heavy nylon and its 8" height was just tall enough to support the ankle. It was designed for warfare in the deserts of the Middle East. He swallowed, thinking of Liz wearing a similar pair of boots. The bitterness of bile hit his mouth; he swallowed and took a breath.

The laces were tied and the boot was sitting upright. He looked at the top of the boot, and his eyes lied to him. His brain didn't believe it. He shifted his focus to the toe of the boot and saw a drop of dried blood. The tale that his eyes had whispered drifted to him. He looked back at the top of the boot, and his lungs sucked in a breath and froze. About a half-inch of somebody's leg was sticking out of it. For a brief moment, he thought he was stuck in some strange madness and was looking at Liz's leg. He looked at the flashlight in his hand, and it brought him back to reality.

"Jesus," Cove said, raising the pitch of his voice, "no wonder he's gettin' flown out." He grimaced and spat. "That had to hurt." He looked at the sheriff. "Shouldn't you have sent it with him?"

"It ain't his," Mendiola said. "This is somebody else's. The guy Jeff was chasing had both feet when we loaded him in the ambulance."

Cove shined his light towards the wrecked vehicle and saw that it was a pickup truck turned upside down. He could see Deputy Jeff Jenks stooped over and running his light through the interior. It took him a moment to recognize it as a newer Ford. The tires on one side were pulled halfway off the rims. His beam found the inverted white California license plate. *At least they're not locals,* he thought.

"The rest of this guy still inside?"

Mendiola gave a slight snort. "That's the thing. There was just the driver."

Cove shined his light across the field that had long ago been a river bottom. It was a flat agricultural field with a mixture of grass and alfalfa. "There's got to be somebody else out here." He said it while realizing there was no possibility of the short vegetation concealing a body.

"Jenks and I thought the same. We've been all over this field."

Cove shined his light along the path where the vehicle had come off the highway, hit the fence line, cut several large gouges out of the field and had started its violent bouncing roll to where it lay. There were pieces of truck, shattered glass, an open suitcase and a blue plastic cooler scattered along the crash line. He turned to Fred. "He's gotta be under the truck."

"We looked."

Cove refocused on the boot thinking; *this is a death*

scene. "Where's Erdos? Shouldn't the coroner be here?"

"I called him," Mendiola said. "He's in California. Daughter's getting married. I'm deputy coroner right now."

Cove glanced up and caught Fred's face, lit by the flashlight reflecting off the field. The deputy was rubbing his ear. "Does he know I'm here?"

Mendiola's eyes squinted, and he lowered his voice. "Not yet." He said it in a tone that could have been interpreted as humor. "He wanted me to get a temperature on this thing. Said it might be the only way to determine time of death. That's why I called you. Seen you do it with that deer." Mendiola shrugged and smiled. "Where the hell am I supposed to get a thermometer at this time of night, Charley?"

Cove looked back down at the leg sticking out of the boot and massaged his temple. "I stuck the thermometer in the thigh on the deer 'cause that's where they got all the data from. I'm pretty sure on humans, it's done in the liver." Cove dropped to one knee, feeling a dull pain in his thigh. He leaned in, looking at the stump and canted his head. "I can't believe this'll work; there's not enough mass." Besides, he thought, *who in the hell has done temperature work on dead feet inside boots?*

"Maybe not, but Erdos wants a temp." Mendiola cleared his throat. "Now you understand why I got you out here."

"Yeah, you need my thermometer." He looked back at the stump and leaned down. His face was about twelve inches away from what was left of a lower leg. There were two cross-sectioned bones surrounded by muscle, connective tissue and skin. Everything was severed at what looked like a perfect right angle. There was no fatty tissue and he couldn't see a sock. He could see a few dark curly hairs on the death-pale skin. Cove's flashlight was in his left hand. He cupped his right hand and brought the air from around the severed limb to his flared nose and sniffed. It didn't have the earth-like scent of the death that he was used to dealing with. This was different–a paler, more blanched odor. His mouth went dry. "I don't smell any decomp." Shining his light back to the severed leg, he studied the trauma. There was no hanging tissue, and the muscles looked moist and fresh.

After a minute of silence, Mendiola spoke. "I guess we could just slip the thermometer along that bone."

"Yeah, but it's too late for that. This happened yesterday or maybe the day before."

Mendiola leaned down. "How can you tell?"

"Fly eggs." Cove answered. "It's got some flyblow on it."

"Oh bullshit," Mendiola objected, "It's been out here for more than an hour. The goddamned flies musta found this while we were working on the driver. You can't hardly gut a deer in this kinda weather without fighting flys."

"You've never poached a deer at night." Cove shook his head. "Flies don't lay eggs in the dark. They do it during the day." He pulled the thermometer from his shirt pocket, removed the stainless tube and set the glass instrument on top of the broken fence post with the bulb protruding into the air. For a brief moment, he wondered if his friend was talking about skinning a deer killed before the frosts of fall. Before the season opened. He dismissed the thought. "I used insect evidence on a sheep case a couple of years ago for time of death. It gave me the day."

"Erdos is still gonna want a temperature." Mendiola said.

"Either way, we need an air temp." Cove reached to his pant pocket, pulled out a folded knife and flicked it open. "It affects how fast these things hatch."

He used it as a pointer despite its broken-off tip. "Look here. See that little wiggler next to this egg cluster?"

Mendiola leaned in. Both their heads were within inches of the severed appendage. The deputy studied where Cove was pointing. He could see an ivory-colored grub smaller than a grain of rice next to a cluster of even smaller white fly eggs. "Okay, the flies have been on it."

Without taking his eyes of the tiny squirming larvae, Cove continued. "You and I'd call this little guy a maggot. The forensic entomologist that gave us this stuff at in-service called 'em instars. They have different stages. This is the first instar stage. It may put this back another day, I don't know for sure. I can give her a call. But for right now, I think this is from yesterday." Cove heard Mendiola stand up and saw that he had his phone out.

He looked back at Cove. "I'm calling Erdos."

Cove looked down at the stump, pulled out a pair of blue nitrile gloves that were stuck in his pant pocket and put them on. He picked up the thermometer and read the air temperature. *Sixty-two degrees.* He started to push the thermometer into the leg between the tibia and the muscle. His gut started to twist and he stopped. For a moment, he had to look away. He swallowed his revulsion and got back to his job.

The instrument's bulb had exposed a mark on the

bone. He leaned in closer and studied it. It was the kerf of a saw blade, an unfinished cut. The mark was almost a quarter of an inch wide. Re-examining the flat cross-section of the bones, he could see parallel scratches. He eased back, squinted his eyes and stared. The knot in his stomach tightened as he thought of a similar cut he had seen on a moose carcass. *Jesus–a chainsaw,* Cove thought. *Some bastard cut this guy's leg off with a chainsaw.* After a moment he pushed the thermometer down into the muscle tissue next to the bone. It went in too easily.

He sat back on the heels of his boots, turned off his light, and absorbed the reality of what sat in front of him. A half-moon looked down and pulled his mind away. It had just come up over the Lost River Range and brought back another moonlit summer night when he was a kid, listening to his grandfather talking to an old Ktunaxa–or Kootenai–friend. He could remember the aged man's face as wrinkled as a piece of dried sagebrush. The flames of a campfire lit his sunken eyes. He recalled the old man telling his grandfather that the moon and the sun were brothers and that they produced the powerful life force of all earthly things. He could see his grandfather staring into the flames, nodding slightly and poking the red-hot coals with a piece of willow.

Down by the river, a fox barked. A great horned owl boomed back. Cove listened and waited for more. Nothing spoke. A fox, an owl, and death all under the same moon. What was in play along the river, and how was it related to the problem at hand?

Mendiola spoke into his phone with half of his face

illuminated by the moon, the other side as black as the shadow of the cliffs above the river. "I've got Charlie Cove out here, and he says the boot and the foot have been around for a day or two. It's flyblown."

There was a pause, and Cove couldn't quite make out the other side of the conversation. He focused on the river bottom, listening for its people to talk. A cloud obscured the moon, and the night became darker.

Mendiola continued in an even voice. "You said we needed to take a temperature. I didn't have a thermometer. He does this stuff on game all the time."

Still kneeling, Cove exhaled and turned his headlamp on, focusing the beam on the toe of the boot. He studied the dark rust-colored drop of dried blood. It was the shape of a teardrop. Perhaps a half-inch in length and a quarter of an inch wide. There were tiny droplets of blood spatter that had bounced off the main part of the stain, facing away from the laces on the boot. He turned off the headlamp and let the moon take back the darkness. Tilting his head, he considered the blood. *It had to have come from him, not somebody else.*

Cove allowed his investigative mind to visualize a chainsaw ripping through someone's pant covered leg. The bitter taste came back in his mouth. He let the horror play twice. Once with the guy still alive and once while dead. He considered the carnage that should have been left in each scenario. The first version ran with blood spraying from the saw. He could not envision it without the victim being unconscious or immobilized. In the second version– the person being deceased–there was tissue spinning off the saw, but no blood.

Turning the light back on, he swallowed back the bitterness in his mouth and touched his chipped molar with his tongue. He focused the light at the gap between the top of the boot and the exposed skin. There was no blood. He studied the open face of the wound for bits of thread or cloth and couldn't see any. The muscle tissue was as bloodless and unbruised as a clean piece of meat in a butcher's shop. *Postmortem.* Cove nodded, settled on the second version, and let out a breath.

He boxed up the graphic visions and pushed them deep into a corner of his brain, turned off his light and canted his good ear towards Mendiola. The sheriff had become quiet. Cove could hear Coroner Dave Erdos talking loudly on the other end but couldn't make out the words. The moon lit up Mendiola's badge; a bright light on a dead-dark night. The deputy was looking down at the ground, his lips were pursed, his eyes were closed, and his big fingers looked like they were squeezing the juice from an orange.

There was only one word that Cove heard from the other side of the conversation. The word bulleted into his ear, and he felt the blood pulsing in his fingertips. Looking towards the river, he listened for the owl.

Chapter 2

Cove sipped his coffee and looked at the empty cafe. He was sitting at the very end of the room, facing the cash register and front door. The waitress was putting on a second pot of coffee. She was middle-aged and thin with wrinkled pale skin.

He looked outside; twilight was breaking. His patrol truck sat by itself in the parking lot. Nothing was moving in the town of Challis. No headlights cut through the dwindling darkness. He checked his iPhone and ensured the mute button was back on, confirming he hadn't missed a call.

He looked into the dark steaming coffee and closed his eyes. His mind took him back to the crash and the severed foot. The temperature he'd taken was bothering him. It didn't make sense. The temperature of the foot, inside the boot, had been fifty-one degrees, eleven degrees cooler than the air. He'd taken the temperatures about an hour after the accident. The air temperature had to be at its nadir or close to it, certainly not to the point of warming up. How could the foot have gotten colder than the outside air?

He focused on what he'd seen of the boot and regretted not studying the sole. He was sure it had a story to tell. At one time, it'd belonged to the U.S. Army. Had the guy been in the military? He thought about the irony of someone surviving deployments to the sands of the Middle East and ending up with his severed foot laying in a farmer's field in the middle of Idaho. He guessed that thousands of these boots had been sold as surplus. He'd seen them on eBay and in a used store in Missoula. Except for size, they were identical to those issued to Liz. The boots she'd died in. Cove looked up and blinked.

Mendiola stood over him with a smile. "You're losing your touch. Lucky I'm not Blackfeet. I'd be giving you a haircut."

"They're dog eaters." Cove frowned. "I was thinking about the foot."

"Your leg bothering you?" Mendiola asked.

Cove realized he was massaging his thigh. "Not really."

Mendiola sat down facing Cove. The waitress appeared and slid a coffee mug and glass of ice water in front of the sheriff. The harsh smell of cigarette smoke clung to her. She set a stainless carafe near Cove.

"Who wrecked?" she asked with a raspy voice.

"Some guy from outta town," Mendiola answered.

"Thank God," she said, and walked back towards the kitchen.

Cove filled his cup from the carafe, dumped three packs of sugar into it and stirred it with a spoon.

Mendiola picked up the water glass, took several swallows and stared at Cove. "When the hell you start lacing your coffee with sugar?"

"This morning."

Mendiola continued to study him for a moment and then went on. "The vehicle was rented in Phoenix. It's entered stolen in NCIC a week ago."

"Is that why Jeff lit him up?"

Mendiola raised his eyebrows. "No, he had a taillight out. You oughta make sure your lights are working if you're driving a hot rig."

Cove noticed a truck pull into the parking lot. It was Jenks's patrol rig. The deputy parked next to Cove's Fish and Game pickup and turned his lights off.

Jenks let the truck idle and thought about the graveyard shift that should be coming to an end. Sciatic pain ran down his leg, and he pulled a bottle of Tylenol off the dash, dumped three into his palm, and swallowed them dry. The clock on the dashboard told him that his wife was getting ready to head to the town's other cafe where she worked as a fry cook. He pulled out his phone and was about to call her. In a few minutes, she'd probably hear about his pursuit and how it had ended. He massaged his eyes and temples and realized she'd hear about the foot, too.

His mind flashed back to when he'd gotten to the wreck. The driver was lying face down in a puddle of blood inside the overturned truck. Each breath the guy took had ended with a snort. He had been horrified that the guy was drowning in his own blood. He recalled thinking that he had been a fool to crawl over the broken bloody glass that was strewn inside the cab. The guy could have diseases. He knew that if he rolled him over, he could cause permanent paralysis if he had a spinal injury. After listening to a few more breaths, he rolled him, attempting to keep his head in line with his spine. The guy's breathing was still labored, but the snorting stopped. Jenks recalled staying in the upturned cab, staring at the guy's off-colored skin, thinking each breath would be the end. He remained in the cab until he heard the wail of the ambulance.

Feeling like a towel that had been wrung out, Jenks put his phone back in the pouch on his belt and turned off the engine.

His patrol plan had been to work the highway north of Challis, focusing on patrons closing down the three bars. He'd made several traffic stops and written one driver for going eighteen over the posted sixty-five. He had performed field sobriety tests on two drivers. None had quite reached the level of loss of muscle control that he needed to make an arrest. One had been marginal and he now regretted not hauling him in. If he'd hooked him and the guy had blown over the legal .08 blood-alcohol level, the lengthy booking process would have kept him off patrol, and he never would have lit up the Ford. There wouldn't be a nearly dead Mexican in a hospital a hundred miles away, and there wouldn't be somebody's foot in a paper bag in the dispatch refrigerator.

Cove felt the cool morning air enter the room. He glanced up and saw Jenks come through the doorway. The deputy's charcoal uniform shirt had a wet-looking smudge on his left arm, and the tails looked hastily tucked. When he sat down next to Cove, his leather gun belt creaked.

Cove grabbed an empty mug, filled it from the carafe and slid it in front of Jenks.

Cove liked the deputy but had never felt he'd last in law enforcement. The guy would work his eight-hour shift, and then cranked out another eight hours working on his father-in-law's ranch. Charlie had once asked him what he'd been working on, and assumed he'd get a rundown on a burglary or some such deputy story, but Jenks's eyes had lit up, and he'd talked Cove's ear off about the coming calving season as if it were his only job.

He and Jeff had worked together on several calls. He was as honest as a dictionary. Cove had a sense that Jeff's last lie had been something to do with a fat man passing out gifts from a red sled. He'd seen that quality backfire on him. Practically speaking, he was too honest. The deputy seemed to believe that everybody else—including people he'd just handcuffed—were just like him and wouldn't lie. He was famous for believing any story.

Mendiola was staring at the wet spot on Jenks's sleeve. "Tell me that's not cow shit on your shirt."

"It's blood." Jenks brought the mug to his lips and sucked down half the cup like it was a glass of water. "Any news on him yet?"

"Nothing," Mendiola said.

"I didn't think he'd make the clinic," Jenks said.

The waitress appeared. "You guys get a chance to look at the menu?"

Cove shook his head. "No, but I'll have your number three with whole-wheat toast." The other two added their orders, and the waitress left them alone.

Jenks and Mendiola wore the same dark-blue, almost black, uniform shirts and blue Levi's. The same Custer County Sheriff's patch was attached to the shoulders of their long-sleeved shirts.

Charlie Cove's uniform shirt was dark gray, his jean-like pants were a dark green, and he wore the silver and gold badge of Idaho Fish and Game. His hair was as dark as the black coffee he was drinking, and his skin was almost a Caucasian white, but it was tinged with the tea color of his father's Salish heritage. His eyes were nearly black and framed by an early onset of wrinkles that lied about his still youthful age of thirty-five.

Mendiola was striking. In his stocking feet, he stood 6'3" and weighed over two hundred and fifty pounds. Normally, he was dead serious, but when the dark side of the job overwhelmed him, he'd try to find some humor in it. His short hair was black with gray creeping into his half-inch sideburns. Although he had ten years over Cove, there was only a hint of crow's feet leading from the corners of his face. His eyes held a darkness that seemed to hold back the evil he'd seen on the job. His skin had a slight olive tinge that revealed his Basque inheritance. He was going on twenty-five years with the sheriff's office. For six years he had served as the Chief Deputy of Custer County—second in command of the sheriff. For the last year, he'd run the shop as acting sheriff while the elected sheriff dealt with a diagnosis of multiple sclerosis. With a reasonable certainty, he'd be the next elected sheriff.

Jeff Jenks was the odd man out with short blond hair and blue eyes set in a large head. Cove thought he was probably a Swede. His eyes were set wide and he had puffy cheeks and big ears. A bit heavy set, but not overweight. He always looked like the poster-boy example of a young farmer. Normally his smooth skin and flushed cheeks caused him to look almost too young to be a deputy. He didn't have that problem at the moment.

All three of the officers wore duty belts, weighed down with handguns, extra magazines, handcuffs and other less obvious tools of the trade.

Jenks glanced at Cove. "I didn't realize it was stolen until after the EMTs got there. He was doing eleven over, his taillight was out. I lit him. He stomped on it."

Cove watched his face, struck by the fact that he hadn't asked for this explanation.

Jenks talked as if he had some weight on him. "I was on him just long enough to call in the plate. He looked like he was gonna blow through town so I cut my overheads and started to back off, hoping he'd do the same." The deputy's hands came off the table, and his fingers spread out. "Then his headlights went bouncing off into the field, and it was over." He brought his fingers up to his eyes and stretched the skin of his face. "I thought he was probably DUI."

Mendiola nodded. "Probably is. They'll draw blood."

Jenks shrugged his shoulders. "I think he was high. I found a bindle of white powder in the truck. I stuck a pinch in a Nik-G pouch, and it's coke."

Mendiola looked at Jenks and nodded. His voice deepened, and he sounded older. "I think you found that when you were looking for the guy's identity for the docs. Get a warrant for the truck tomorrow. I'm betting Pallid will want Arizona to charge him down there and come get him, but he might want to file paper on him for the cocaine to keep him out of here. Who knows?"

"Aren't you forgetting something?" Cove said. "The elephant's foot in the room."

Mendiola frowned. "We found somebody's foot lying beside the road. Whaddya think our great prosecutor's gonna do with that?" He opened his hands. "It ain't a dead body. I can't even prove it was in the truck."

The three drank their coffee as if they needed an excuse to be quiet.

After a moment Jenks spoke. "I found a DL in the glove box." He pulled a driver's license out of his shirt pocket and set it in front of Mendiola. "I was looking for it when I found the dope. Give me a bit of credit, Fred. If Pallid wants to charge him with possession, it'll stick."

Mendiola studied the license. "Phoenix. Born in fifty-nine." He picked it up, flipped it over, glanced at the backside and set it in front of Cove.

The license was issued by the State of Arizona. The photograph showed a middle-aged Hispanic with black curly hair and a mustache that hid his upper lip. He looked as somber as a concrete block. His name was Marcos Ayala Talavera.

Cove glanced at Jenks. "Is this him?"

"I'm assuming so. Can't say for sure." Jenks frowned. "He got Maytagged. Dumbass wasn't wearing his belt." Jenks put his finger on the date of birth. "Age's about right. I found a VISA card with the same name on it."

"It could be the guy missing the foot," Cove added.

"You run him yet?" Mendiola asked

"Yeah, no wants," Jenks answered. "In fact, nothing other than a speeding ticket."

After a pause, Mendiola's eyes pinched down and he said, "A guy in his fifties, snorting coke, driving around in a stolen vehicle with somebody's foot, who's never been arrested." He shook his head. "Hard to swallow. In fact, I don't fuckin' believe it. Somebody shoulda popped him for something."

Mendiola looked at Jenks. "When ya getta chance, Jeff, run him in New Mex and California. Maybe Nevada. He's gotta have something. It'd be nice to find a print card somewhere."

The waitress came out of the kitchen juggling three plates and delivered them to the table. "Is the guy going to be okay? I heard they flew him out?"

"I don't know," Mendiola said.

"He wasn't wearing his seat belt," Jenks added.

She looked at the blond deputy and frowned. Her wrinkles got deeper. "The only reason my sister's alive is she wasn't wearing her belt when she went in the river."

Mendiola didn't respond to the bait that he knew had been thrown his way. The waitress headed back to the kitchen with a suggestion of attitude.

"She was drunker than a skunk," Mendiola whispered. "She's still pissed I arrested her."

The three jumped into their food. After a few bites, Cove looked at Mendiola. "So what'd Erdos have to say?"

"I'm gonna have to have another heart to heart with that asshole," Mendiola said. "I don't get him."

Cove thought about the one conversation he'd had with Erdos. He'd been working a series of deer killings that were connected to a burglary. He and Mendiola had interviewed Erdos during the investigation—as the coroner, not as a suspect—and he'd become openly hostile towards Cove. At the time, he'd interpreted it as a dislike for the game department. He now believed it was something uglier.

"Besides the fact that you can't figure him out, what'd he say?" Cove asked.

"He wanted to make sure you took a temperature." Mendiola's hand came up and covered his mouth and palmed his whiskers. "Told me to refrigerate it and get it to the pathologist in Pocatello." His eyes went down to his breakfast.

Cove studied the sheriff for a moment. "Knock off the BS, Fred. What the shit did he say?" Cove leaned in. "The one word I heard him speak was Indian. What's that got to do with this?" Cove turned to Jenks. "What do you think, Jeff? About Indians being out along the road looking at somebody's foot?" There was no hint of humor in Cove's voice.

Jenks seemed to shrink. Mendiola didn't blink. His voice softened. "Charlie, knock it off. You wanna be pissed at Erdos, go ahead." There was a long pause as Mendiola studied Cove's face. "He thinks you got the temperatures mixed up. He called me back and said that the foot had to be warmer than the air temperature."

Cove felt a flush in his cheeks. He knew there was still more to the phone conversation than what he was being told. He took a piece of bacon, dipped it into a puddle of egg yolk and put it in his mouth. He chewed for a moment and washed it down with hot coffee.

"I didn't look real hard at all the stuff that blew outta the truck, but I saw a cooler, and I saw a bag of ice." Cove sounded like a growling dog that might bite. "What I didn't see was any beer."

Jenks shrugged and looked confused. "There wasn't any."

"That's why the foot was cold," Cove said, still with the growl in his voice. "It was in the cooler."

Mendiola shook his head. "Maybe he'd eaten his dinner out of it."

"Any food in the cab?" Cove asked.

Jenks answered. "Half a bag of Doritos and two empty Red Bulls."

"Maybe the ice was for the Red Bulls," Mendiola said.

Cove shook his head. "Then the cooler woulda been inside the cab."

"It doesn't make sense, Charlie," Mendiola said. "Hauling somebody's foot around in a cooler in the middle of the night."

Cove responded. "Nor does it make any sense finding a foot sitting beside the highway that somebody cut off with a chainsaw. That's what this job is about. Making sense out of things that don't make sense."

Jenks turned his head towards Cove and gave him a puzzled look. Mendiola's head froze, and his mouth went into a curious contortion. The sheriff quit chewing his food, stopped by what he'd just heard.

"The foot was colder than the air," Cove said. "The only explanation is that it had to have been in the cooler with ice. And before that the flies got to it, and it was warm enough for the first generation to hatch." Cove's cadence changed, and he spit out the words, "Evidence doesn't lie."

"Christ," Mendiola said, shaking his head still thinking about the chainsaw comment. "Why are you pissed at me?"

"You're going to have to figure this one out." Cove said.

"No shit," Mendiola replied. "This town'll spit me over a fire if I don't." He was looking out the window, and it sounded like he was talking more to himself than to Cove or Jenks. "I gotta figure it out—where the damn thing came from, and how the hell it ended up here." He met Cove's eyes. "It isn't like one of your deer shot and left in the snow. These people ain't gonna blow this off."

Cove took another bite of food. Mendiola had sounded like he thought a deer case was nothing; like a twisted beer can dropped in an alley. Cove was tired, and that's the way he took it. He felt his ears turning red, and it brought him back to what the coroner had said. "As far as Erdos and his dislike for my ilk, he's exactly what I'd expect in a county named after Custer." Cove spit the name out as if he'd found a fly in his coffee.

Jenks felt the air chilling. He stood up and said, "I gotta pee," and headed towards the men's room.

Mendiola studied Cove until Jenks was out of hearing. "Don't let Erdos get under your skin." He wiped his mouth with a napkin, his eyes never leaving Cove's. "You seem God-awful pissed at Jeff and I... and Charlie, I gotta tell ya. Your half-breed ass's been looking awful sorry lately."

Cove's eyes flicked to his coffee, and he rubbed his temple for a moment. His response was subdued. "My ass is biracial... Yeah, I've been feeling a bit pissy."

"Been getting any sleep?"

"Until you called." And he thought of the dream.

Chapter 3

He was sitting in the darkened room, listening. A sliver of light snuck in through the drapes from the parking lot. A closing door shuddered down the hall. The red digital clock next to the bed seemed frozen. A soft double knock on the door caused him to jump. He got up, pulled the cervical collar off, slid it under the bed with his foot and limped silently across the room. He put his eye to the viewer, studied the person for a moment, exhaled and unlocked the door.

A small middle-aged Hispanic male stepped through the door dragging a wheeled black suitcase. He closed the door and gave the older man a hug. "Cómo está, mi amigo?"

"Me duele un poco, pero estoy bien. Thank you for getting here so quickly. I need to get on with our business... Trajiste las pastillas? The oxy?"

"Si," he said, nodding at the bag. He handed him a set of keys.

"Es a Dodge Durango, color azul. Las placas son de Oregon." He opened the door, glanced out into the hallway and turned back inside. "Orar a la Santa Muerte por mí." And he was gone.

He wheeled the bag into the room and found he was too weak to lift it onto the luggage rack. He laid it flat on the floor, kneeled down and unzipped it. Despite the limited light in the room, he could see clothing, a shoe box and a soft duffel bag. He lifted the lid on the shoe box and confirmed it was full of cash.

Digging around in the clothing, he found a black 9mm Beretta, drew the slide partway back and felt the loaded round in the ejection port with his index finger. He let the slide go back into battery and slid the weapon under the pillow on the bed. He pulled out the black nylon duffel and set it gently on the covers. He ran his palms over the top of it as if he were feeling the curves of a woman's breasts through a silk nightgown. He unzipped the bag and looked in. His Santisimo stared back and he felt his power returning.

The man pulled a heavy black votive candle out of the bag, set it on the nearby cherry desk and lit it. There was a mirror on the wall above the table and the room jumped alive with the glow. Examining his reflection, he saw an unfamiliar battered face.

He pulled the effigy out of the bag and reverently placed it beside the candle. From the black hood of her robe, her fleshless bone-colored skull smiled back, lit by the flickering flame. Red faceted jewels stared from her eye orbits. In the bones of her left hand, she held a long-shafted curved scythe. Her right held a globe to her womb. A small unblinking owl perched on her forearm.

He pulled a gold-colored fifth of mescal from the bag. A pale grub lay at the bottom of the bottle. He retrieved a glass from the bathroom, poured two fingers into it and set it reverently to the left of his saint.

He bowed his head slightly and said, "Santa Madre de la Muerte, guard me from los peligros."

Taking a long pull from the bottle, he closed his eyes and felt the liquid heat burn down his esophagus and into his stomach. He set the uncapped bottle on the desk, laid down on the bed and closed his eyes.

As the candle flame danced, Santísimo Muerte, the Holy Saint of Death, watched as **Juan Torres Rodriguez** fell into a deep sleep and his enemies walked into his dreams.

Chapter 4

The vibration of the phone in Cove's shirt pocket startled him. He pulled over on the dirt road and wondered how he had cell service this far up Morgan Creek. He pulled it out of his pocket and saw Julie's name on the screen. His stomach constricted. The phone vibrated again. He hesitated and then pushed the power button twice, declining the call. He put the phone back in his pocket and looked at the dark red rimrock at the top of the ridge. It was a fumbled mess of igneous rock.

When he looked back up the road, he noticed a parked vehicle sitting a quarter mile or so away. He reached for the 10 X 50 Pentax binoculars on the passenger seat and brought them to his eyes. It was a silver Suburban SUV, facing away from him and parked on the left side of the road. Cove was grateful for the distraction.

Charlie's plan for that day had been to drive up to the summit of Morgan Creek and look for a bear bait that he'd received a tip on. The caller had said that somebody was using deer carcasses for bait. Baiting was legal for bears but using game animals wasn't. The description of where the bait was located had sounded familiar. Cove doubted that the bear hunter had shot the deer. He believed the guy had probably picked the carcasses up from the edge of the highway. It wasn't the biggest crime in the world, but it was something that he needed to look into. He was several miles away from the location described by the caller. The vehicle wasn't in a place he'd expect to find a bear bait.

His goal for his patrol area was to make everyone in it believe they couldn't blink without him knowing. It was an impossible objective, since he was charged to protect the wildlife that lived on nearly two thousand square miles of rugged land, most of which was administered by either the U.S. Forest Service or the Bureau of Land Management. About ten percent of his patrol area was private ground that had been homesteaded well over a hundred years ago. Almost all of the private ground was under some form of irrigation and tied to cattle ranching.

The rocky south facing sagebrush hill to his right was public land managed by the BLM. Everything to his left that flanked the creek was private. For about the first fifty yards, it was an almost impenetrable line of willows fed by the water of Morgan Creek. The land was fenced, but the owner hadn't taken the time to post it with no-trespassing signs. On the far side of the willows was green irrigated pasture and perhaps an eighth of a mile away–marked by a barbed wire fence and sagebrush–was national forest. The terrain on that side of the drainage consisted of steep spur ridges that fed up to mountains covered with a forest predominated by Douglas fir but spiced with patches of quaking aspen.

As Cove neared the vehicle, he realized it wasn't a Suburban. It was GMC's Cadillac model called the Escalade, and it was wearing Washington plates. Other than a thin layer of dust on the silver paint, it looked new and smacked of money. It was parked just off the road, parallel to the barbed wire fence that was set into the side of the thick jungle-like band of willows. Cove parked across the road and made the assumption that the owner was somewhere along the creek fishing. He wrote the plate number down on a notebook that was laying on the dashboard.

He got out of his vehicle and whispered to Annie to stay. He noted there were no footprints in the dust below the Escalade's passenger door. Walking by the front of the vehicle, he felt the heat coming from the engine. There was a fresh-looking empty bubble wrapper below the driver's door that looked like someone had pulled some fishing tackle out of it.

Cove looked towards the creek. Beyond the barbed wire fence, a game trail led into the red willows. It was the only way for a human to get through. The fence's top wire was stretched and hanging. A clump of tan elk hair was wrapped around one of its barbs. Cove put both hands on the top wire, pushed it down and carefully swung his uniform pant leg over the barbs. He swung his other leg over and when he let his weight off the fence, it let out a loud squeak. *So much for stealth,* Cove thought.

He eased down the game trail, pushing the willows off his face. The riparian jungle smelled like green wood and composting leaves. For a few feet, the trail was soft black soil. It had numerous old elk tracks topped off by a set of fresh boot prints headed towards the waterway. After about sixty yards, the willows turned to a strip of foot-high lush grass along the bank of Morgan Creek, which was clear as bottled water and as wide as a one-lane road.

Across the creek were more willows and the confluence of a smaller side creek that Cove believed was the West Fork. The two channels formed a perfect pool for trout. But to the warden's surprise, there was no angler. He looked into the pool and saw the white bellies of three dead fish. All three were about four inches long. Two were at the bottom of the pool and one was a few yards up.

He heard a bird sing, "chick-a-dee-zee-zee" from downstream, causing him to look up the creek. There was a bent line of grass that disappeared around a bend. He started to follow but found a white Styrofoam worm container laying on its side in the vegetation. He stooped and took the lid off. A cluster of moist nightcrawlers flinched at the intrusion of daylight. With the movement came the sense that he wasn't alone. He put the lid back on and continued to follow the fresh foot path. He got about thirty feet when an older man stepped out of the brush and acted surprised to see him. His acting performance was not worthy of an Oscar. The guy had sandy hair, was sunburned and wore fresh blue jeans and a long-sleeved light-colored turquoise fishing shirt. He looked like he belonged on a golf course.

"Hello," Cove said and held up the white container. "Lose your bait?"

"I'm not fishing." The man spat it out with an air of finality.

Cove studied him for a moment. He didn't like where this was going, and he caught the guy's eyes flick back into the willows followed by a half-step towards the warden.

"I didn't say you were, but if you're not fishing, I gotta ask; what're you doing down here in this jungle?"

"Nothing... just looking around."

"Where's your fishing gear?"

The man's eyes drifted for a second time. "I told you, I'm not fishing."

"Whose worms are these?" Again, Cove held up the bait container.

"I told you they weren't mine."

Cove guessed that it may have been a year since another human had walked down through the willows to this pool, but he kept his mouth shut.

He stepped past the man and looked where the guy's eyes had drifted to. There was a graphite G. Loomis fishing rod with a gold-colored Shimano spinning reel that was jammed into the vegetation. He reached down and picked it up. A red and white Mepp's spinner was tied to the line, and a fresh chunk of worm was woven into the three barbs of the treble hook.

"Nice outfit," Cove said, lowering his voice. "Fishing without a license is no big deal."

"That's not my pole."

Cove canted his head and the edges of his mouth came up slightly.

"Who else is with you?"

The man shook his head. "Nobody."

Cove pointed into the clear pool. "And you didn't catch those three fish either."

The guy didn't hesitate. "They were here when I walked in."

When he said it, Cove watched the man's eyes widen and his hands come up in a gesture of openness. He believed the guy had finally spoken a needle of truth, but the three dead fish didn't make any sense from the picture that was in front of him.

"You don't have a fishing license, do you?"

"I ain't fishing."

"I'll take that as a no. But I'll need to see some identification."

"Why?"

Cove felt his breathing pick up.

"Let me make sure you understand." He said it slightly rolling his head. "I'm a game warden. You figured that out. You say you don't have a fishing license and I have reason to believe you've been fishing."

The guy started to speak and Cove raised his hands gesturing for him to be quiet. "Since you don't have a fishing license, I need to see your driver's license or some kind of ID. End of discussion."

Cove considered what he had. Worms, a fishing rod and a bullshit story. What he was missing was actually seeing the guy in the act of fishing or hearing an admission. It was all circumstantial. It wasn't a bad case—any six-person jury in Custer County would know the guy had been fishing—but it was a case he didn't want to turn over to a work-shy prosecutor.

The man pulled a wallet out of his back pocket and produced his driver's license. Cove stepped over, took the license and glanced at it.

"Mr. Peterson, either this rod—and it's a damn fine one—belongs to you or it belongs to someone else. If you deny it's yours, I'm going to tag it, and if no one claims it, it'll be sold at a state auction next spring." Cove shrugged. "If you fess up, I'll photograph your rod, give you a ticket for fishing-without and you can go on your way with your gear."

The guy shook his head and snipped, "Ain't mine."

Cove exhaled and wrote the man's personal information down on a notebook he'd pulled from his shirt pocket. He handed back the license and said, "Travel safe."

The guy glanced at the fishing rod in Cove's hand and headed up the game trail towards the road. Cove heard him mumble something indiscernible as he disappeared into the willows.

Cove thought about what had just happened. The rod and reel appeared to be new. The outfit was worth nearly $300, maybe more. The ticket would have cost him less than half of that. If he'd purchased a two-day non-resident fishing license, the cost would have been $20, and the ensuing conversation could have resulted in a likable meeting for both men. Instead, Cove had a bad taste in his mouth, and he assumed the other guy had something similar or worse.

He looked back in the pool at the three dead fish. He still half-believed the guy had told him the truth about them. But more likely, they died from rough handling while being unhooked, and he didn't have a theory of what else would have killed them.

He reached in, feeling the freeze of the creek and grabbed the closest one. Its green back was camouflaged with black spots. A garnet colored streak along its lateral line was overlaid by several blue-gray parr marks. Its belly was as white as the cumulus clouds in the sky. He rolled the fish over in his hand. There wasn't a mark on it. If an otter or a mink had killed the fish, there would have been teeth marks. But it was a moot point, since the animal would have eaten it. He opened the fish's mouth and looked for damage caused by a hook but couldn't see any. The gills were red and vibrant. This fish was a perfect example of a healthy looking juvenile rainbow–except it was dead. He put it back in the water and caught the other one. It looked like the first fish's sibling. Cove couldn't find any marks on it or in its mouth. He pulled a knife out of his pocket, flicked the blade open with his thumb, made a cut from the fish's vent up to its gills and pulled the digestive tract out. He found the small white stomach and opened it up with a lengthwise slit. It was full of tiny black mayfly nymphs.

Cove slipped the fish back into the water. It drifted with the current for a moment before stopping on the bottom. The third fish was farther out and would have required wading. He didn't believe it would look any different that the first two. He knew a mink or an otter would find the fish and eat them. What he didn't know was why they were dead.

He heard the Escalade start and head up the Morgan Creek road. Cove emptied the worms into the grass and pulled the rod apart to make it easier to snake through the willows. When he got to the road, he picked up the open bubble pack that had been laying by the Escalade. It was a Mepp's brand that matched the spinner on the rod.

He greeted Annie, dug out a seizure tag and wired it to the reel. He put it, the empty worm container and the Mepp's wrapper behind his seat.

Cove continued up Morgan Creek, thinking about the dead fish. Whirling disease came to mind. He didn't know much about it, but he knew it was an introduced parasite that killed juvenile rainbows.

His radio crackled with Mendiola's voice. "731, Custer."

Cove picked up the mike and answered. Mendiola asked him to give him a call when he had cell service. He turned around, and five minutes later he was back at the spot where he'd gotten the call from Julie.

He pulled over, noticed the phone had two bars and checked for phone messages. There were two calls from the sheriff's office but no messages. He called Mendiola's cell. The deputy picked up on the second ring.

"You were right," Mendiola explained. "The lab found DNA in the cooler that matched the foot."

"Good," Cove said. "Pallid agree to hold him on the dope charge?"

"The bastard boogied. Had some help."

"He fled the hospital?"

"They moved him outta the ICU. He had a visitor, and the next thing they knew, the room was empty."

"How the hell did that happen?" Cove asked.

"He wasn't under arrest. If I'd done that, his hospital bill woulda been on the county. I was gonna have him hooked for the coke on his way out the door by Bonneville County." Mendiola groaned. "He didn't have a pot to piss in. No shoes, no vehicle, nothing. How the hell was he gonna rabbit? Anyway, I need you to come into the office."

"It'll have to wait. I'm working on something up Morgan Creek."

"There's an ISP detective here who needs to talk to you."

"About what?"

"The foot. I asked the troopers for help. We haven't had a homicide in three years. Now we've got a severed foot and no body. I think this is the weirdest thing I've ever worked on. It's so far out of the box, I don't even know where to begin. No witnesses. No crime scene. No missing person. Where the hell am I supposed to start? Anyway, he wants to talk to you."

"About the temperatures?"

"No, but do me a favor and come on in."

"Who is it?"

"Wayne McGee."

Cove looked at his phone and came close to hanging up. McGee had been one of two state detectives who had been assigned to investigate the level of force he'd used on Leo Terzi. McGee had made it clear during a long day of questioning that he believed that the situation would have resolved itself had Cove not decided to "jump the gun" as he'd labeled it. Cove also believed that had Mendiola not stood up for him during the inquisition, he could have been looking for a job.

Cove frowned and brought the phone up to his ear. "It'll take me an hour or so."

He hung up and chewed his lip for a moment. Investigating the bear bait *could* wait another day; that wasn't an issue. His Salish roots put wildlife and humans on the same bar. But he understood that crimes against people would always be pushed ahead of wildlife.

He'd felt conflicted many times–especially with family. His mother's relatives didn't understand his father's Indian side. His Salish relatives felt out of place when his mother's family was around. The one Thanksgiving he recalled with both sides at their house was a collision. Everybody got along, but it felt like two pieces of sandpaper rubbing against each other.

Internally he called this struggle his Jekyll and Hyde. He just couldn't put a finger on which side of his multi-cultured blood was the Hyde. Sometimes he thought it was his white side that was causing the friction, and sometimes he believed it was his native blood and its ties to the earth that caused the problem. It seemed to flip flop from one to the other. Even though he had grown up on the rez, he felt like he understood the modern-white culture much better than his Salish side. He hadn't wanted to be Indian. He'd wanted to be white. His father had drowned while Cove was in high school. The death drew him and his grandfather closer, and the old man's spirituality had helped him deal with his loss.

When he'd told his grandfather he'd applied for game warden jobs in Montana and Idaho, he'd seen the man's jaw take a set and his eyes withdraw. Cove was sure the reaction had come from lingering feelings left from the Swan Valley Massacre of 1908 when four tribal members–including a 13 year old boy–had been gunned down in a hunting camp by a Montana game warden. The tribal members had been exercising their off-reservation hunting treaty rights and had even purchased state hunting licenses in an attempt to avoid trouble. Even after a hundred years, the incident still haunted the tribe. He had never talked to his grandfather about it, but the man was old enough to have heard the story firsthand from the four women who had survived by running to the brush on that bloody day.

After he'd accepted the job with Idaho and was packing to leave, his grandfather had stopped by with a box under his arm. It had an old leather bootlace tied around it. He'd handed the package to Charlie and said, "Never forget who you are, where you are from. Someday you'll need these." The old man said it with an air of finality. There was no handshake or hug. He'd handed the tattered box to Charlie, said his few words and walked away. It was the last time Cove saw the man alive.

The silver Escalade sped by, kicking up dust, and it brought him back to Morgan Creek–the phone still in his hand and the call from Mendiola.

What really nagged him was what Mendiola had said about the detective. *He wants to talk to you.* Fred had skirted his question about the specifics. Cove thought about the severed foot. He'd gloved up prior to touching the boot. The detective couldn't get pissy about contamination issues. He'd done what Mendiola had asked. It didn't make sense, and he didn't trust McGee.

He looked down at the phone, swallowed the saliva that flowed into his mouth and selected Julie's speed dial. It didn't ring but went directly to her voicemail. He didn't leave a message.

Cove's eye focused on the owl feather hanging by a piece of leather from the mirror and let his muscles relax. It was whitish with five dark gray crossbars. He thought about the bird's large all-seeing eyes and the silent stealth it hunted with. He felt his pulse slowing. It brought back the memory of the sweat baths he'd taken with his grandfather. Almost always there'd been an owl hooting somewhere along the creek. The two would sit shirtless in the darkness of the sweat lodge, listening to the steam and the owl booming. The heat inside was so hot, it made it hard to breath. Charlie could recall how he'd squeezed his eyelids in the darkness, trying to keep the salty perspiration from burning his eyes. After a while he would hear his grandfather whispering in Salish. He didn't understand the words, but the man had explained that the sweats and prayers were needed for cleansing one's spirit. At the time, he didn't understand the concept of spirit, let alone the need for cleaning it. But now, thinking of the dream, he felt like he was beginning to grasp it.

On the way back to Challis, Cove turned off the highway and drove down to the mouth of Ruby Creek. He hadn't been back since the nightmare that had started the dreams six months ago. The time felt right to confront the black cloud.

He stopped in the shadow of the cottonwoods about fifty yards from where the house trailer had been and stared through the windshield. He could feel the veins pulsing in his neck, and his eardrums had a dull humming.

Whoever had owned the ground had cleaned the trailer up and hauled it away. There was a long rectangle of bare soil where the trailer had been. Not a weed or a blade of grass grew from the soil, as if it had been cursed. There were a few clusters of yellow fiberglass insulation clinging to the line of willows towards the river. The cinderblocks that the trailer had sat on lay in a jumbled pile. Cove pulled past the blocks and down to the edge of the river.

He got out and looked across the channel at the dark cliffs, expecting to hear the rumbling coo of rock pigeons, but the black rock walls were empty. His hackles came up.

He sensed he was being stared at. It was a bad feeling to have in this place. He listened for birds in the nearby cottonwoods, and if there were any, they were quiet. He looked at the river, half expecting Leo Terzi's head to emerge from the depths. Nothing rippled the surface. His nerves were buzzing. He let Annie out of the back of the truck and watched her work the breeze, studying the hair on her back. From out of a nearby clump of willows, a rapid pulsing "key-key-key" screamed. He turned and caught a glimpse of a sharp-shinned hawk flying away with a sparrow in her talons. He exhaled, understanding the quiet that had flooded the area.

Annie walked into the river, drank and then laid down in the shallow water, cooling her belly and watching Cove.

He squatted on the edge of the river and looked into the water. It was about a foot deep and unmoving. Brown cottonwood leaves and rounded rocks carpeted its bottom. His focus shifted to the shimmering surface. He didn't know who he was going to see. He half expected to see his father or his grandfather. Instead he saw an older image of himself. One that looked sullen and empty.

Cove looked around him. The river bank was paved with layers of large gray and bluish cobblestones about the size of small misshaped melons. The rocks had been tumbled smooth by the floods of each winter's runoff since time immemorial. He selected a half dozen cobbles and loaded them in the bed of his truck.

Chapter 5

Cove's phone growled as he pulled behind the courthouse. It was the ringtone he'd programmed in for his boss's number. He slid his finger across the screen as he parked facing the sheriff's office.

"George, what's going on?"

"That's what I was calling to ask. What's this about a severed foot you've gotten involved in?"

"I'm *not* involved, but Wayne McGee wants to talk to me about it. Mendiola's got him working on it."

"You guys musta kissed and made up."

"I don't see that showing in the tarot cards."

Cove explained the night of the callout and what he'd done with the foot. He also told the story about the guy driving the Cadillac who wouldn't own up to fishing without a license, and that the department would have a high-dollar rod to sell at the state auction.

"Which reminds me," Cove said. "Why would there be rainbows dying in Morgan Creek? I found three of them today where that guy was fishing."

"Rough handling from being hooked would be my guess."

"I looked for that," Cove said. "Couldn't see any marks. No blood in the gills."

"You might call one of the fish guys down here and ask them... I caught a guy dumping bleach in Panther Creek years ago. He was using the fish it'd kill for bait over on the Beaverhead. He'd take 'em over in the fall when the browns were spawning. He'd dump a jug of chlorine at the top of a pool and run down with a landing net and scoop 'em up as they floated up. I still wonder how many illegal browns he pulled outta there with them."

"This guy was using a spinner with a glob of worms."

"Give Fisheries a call. They might have some ideas. They need to know about it anyway."

When Cove hung up, he recognized an unmarked blue Jeep Patriot with an extra antenna parked near the entrance of the sheriff's office.

McGee was sitting in front of Mendiola's desk when Cove walked in. The detective stood up and offered his hand to Cove. His palm felt soft, and the smell of cologne hovered around him. He was wearing a dark western-cut sport coat, pressed jeans and a light blue dress shirt with no tie. His reddish hair was slicked over his nearly bald head. He looked like a used car salesman dressed up like a cowboy.

"Good to see you, Charlie."

Cove believed the detective's greeting was close to a lie. He nodded back. "Yeah, it's been a while."

"Glad to see you got rid of your cane."

Cove pulled up a chair and started to sit down.

McGee, still standing, said, "Let's step into the other room. Let Fred get on with being sheriff."

Mendiola gave Cove an odd look and motioned him towards the interview room.

Cove stepped through the doorway, and he heard it close behind him. Something was up; his saliva tasted sour. It was the same room where he'd spent a long day with McGee after he'd been released from the hospital, and it still smelled of sweat. The same gray table sat in the center of the room with three steel chairs. The back wall consisted of a book case filled with old law books and a mishmash of three-ringed binders.

Cove took the first chair at the table, forcing the detective into the corner.

McGee sat down and laid a black nylon notebook on the table. "A lot of officers I've dealt with who've killed somebody in the line of duty have a tough time getting through it. How you doing?"

The detective's words set Cove off balance. He'd never felt like *he'd killed* Leo Terzi. Nobody had ever said he'd killed him. It took him a moment to recover. "I didn't put him in the river. That was his choice. You know they've never recovered him? There's no body. No death certificate. If they find him, maybe Erdos will call it a suicide or a drowning for all I know."

"A duck's a duck," McGee said, raising his hands off the table. "How's Julie Lake doing?"

Again, Cove felt unbalanced. On its face, it was a valid question, since McGee had interviewed Julie at length during the Terzi use-of-force investigation, but he felt McGee had just stepped across the line into his personal life.

"Took a job in Boise," Cove said.

"I thought she was a nice lady."

Cove looked at McGee and considered where this short conversation had gone. The tone of his questions had been cordial but awkward at best. He decided it was a blundered attempt to build rapport at the start of an interview or interrogation or whatever McGee was up to. He'd attempted a similar tactic during his use-of-force investigation. It was a classless scheme to try on another law enforcement officer.

Cove looked up into the corner of the ceiling and saw the camera hidden in the fire alarm staring back at him and he realized McGee had him in this room to put it on the record.

He looked back at McGee. "Fred said you wanted to talk to me about the foot." Cove leaned in towards McGee, squinted one eye and asked, "What can I help you with?"

McGee opened his notebook, pulled out a pen and clicked it. "Did you tell Mendiola and Jenks that the foot had been cut off with a chainsaw?"

Cove's forehead wrinkled. "Yes."

"Did you see a chainsaw at the crash?"

"No." Cove's head dropped a half inch. He folded his arms, leaned back and caught where the interview was going.

"Was there one inside the truck's cab?"

Cove's voice had hit a staccato pace. "Unlike the last time I sat in here with you and your partner, I don't have to be here. I should be out doing my job right now. If you want me to sit here, knock off the monkey shit and don't ask me a question you've already asked."

McGee had the notebook up, and his pen was moving

as if he were taking notes. Cove recalled that the detective had done the same thing during the previous interview he'd endured. He believed McGee was thinking of his next question.

Cove unfolded his arms and leaned over the table. "Look, Wayne," he shook his head, "Do you think I had something to do with this, for Christ's sake?"

McGee looked up from his tablet, licked the corner of his mouth and took a deep breath. "You told Fred it'd been cut off with a chainsaw. Where'd you come up with that shit?"

Cove glanced up at the camera, widened his eyes and brought them back to McGee. "Cause I looked at it. It was done with a chainsaw. I've been running chainsaws since I was in high school. I cut six cord of firewood every year. Three here and three up in Polson for my mother. I worked a moose case last year that someone used a chainsaw on. The cut on the leg bones sticking out of the boot looked just like the ones on the moose legs. You could see the same course scratches on the bone. When I was inserting the thermometer into the leg, I could see where the chain had hit the bone and bounced off. Only a chainsaw blade's that wide." Cove looked up at the clock. "Am I your only suspect?" Cove didn't wait for an answer. "You wanna come look at my chainsaw? Send it off to the lab and see if it's been used to cut up a body? You wanna grab my computer and see if I've been surfing for recipes for boot stew?"

McGee's cheeks looked like they'd been rouged. "Charlie ... I had to ask." He set the notebook on the table. "The pathologist said it was consistent with a chainsaw, and we couldn't understand how you came up with it. It was too much of a coincidence."

Cove moved closer to McGee. "I came up with it the same way the pathologist did. We dig around in dead shit all the time. We do our own necropsies—in your world that means autopsy. I know that's a big word for you. And who is this 'we' shit?" Cove's voice came up in pitch. "Who put you up to this?" Cove looked up at the camera and raised his voice another notch. "Fred, was this your goddamned idea?"

The door opened and Mendiola stepped in, frowning.

"I shoulda asked when you brought it up the other morning. I mentioned it to Wayne. He wanted to ask you face to face. It needed to be asked and answered."

"For Christ's sake," Cove said. "You coulda asked on the phone today or when we were eating breakfast."

Mendiola's face softened, and he gave Cove a slight nod. "You're right, Charlie. I didn't remember you talking about it until I read the pathologist's report. That's when I recalled you saying it'd been whacked off with a chainsaw." He paused. "I'm sorry."

Mendiola looked at McGee. "Show him the hospital photo."

The detective hesitated for a moment and laid his notebook on the table. Opening up the front flap, he exposed a manila envelope. He fished around in it, pulled out a black and white photograph and set it on the table.

McGee frowned at Cove. "This information stays in the room."

The glossy picture showed a slender male pushing a wheelchair. A middle-aged man with disarrayed black hair sat in the chair. He was wearing a cervical collar, and his eye sockets were heavily bruised.

"That's from the hospital video," McGee said. "They didn't get any footage of the vehicle they left in."

Mendiola interjected. "He spent at least a week here in town before the wreck. Jenks found a book of matches in the truck from the Northgate. That's where he stayed. Somebody had to see him here in town." Mendiola popped his knuckles. "I wanna know what he was doing here for a week."

"Maybe a river trip," Cove said with a bit of sarcasm.

"Yeah, a floater," Mendiola said. "Snortin' coke with a sawed-off foot in the back of his truck and doing whitewater shit in a rubber raft."

"Jeff find any more history on him?" Cove asked.

"That's part of the problem. We don't know who he is," McGee said.

"The DL that Jeff found belongs to the guy who supposedly rented the truck." Mendiola said. "Marcos Talavera. They found his body in the desert outside of Phoenix about the time this guy showed up playing tourist here in the middle of nowhere."

"Jesus," Cove said, squinting.

"He used cash at the motel, no credit card. The clerk said he had a fistful of fifties. Used Talavera's identity," McGee added.

"How long had this guy been dead?" Cove asked.

"They think it was the same day the truck was rented," Mendiola explained. "About four days after Jose showed up here. It's still unclear who rented the truck. It could be Jose or Talavera."

"Jose?" Cove asked.

"That's what I've been calling him." Mendiola said.

"Talavera's body missing a foot?" Cove asked.

Mendiola looked at McGee, and Cove caught the detective giving him a slight head shake as if he were saying no.

"Show him." Mendiola turned back to Cove. "They cut off his lips."

Cove screwed his mouth sideways. "Jesus Christ."

"DEA had him listed as an informant," McGee said and flopped out two color photographs. "Keep it in the room."

The top photo was a closeup of a dead man's face. He had a gray-blue tinge to his skin, except for the dried flesh where his lips had been removed. Whoever had done it wasn't a plastic surgeon. The cut was jagged and lopsided. The image of a lipless corpse with a toothy smile was almost too much for Cove's brain. He rubbed his eye lids, flipped the photograph over and looked at the second one. It had been taken from a few yards back. The body lay in the reddish sand of the desert. Two yellow evidence markers stuck up behind the corpse and beyond that was a spiny bush that Cove didn't recognize.

"That's about the nastiest thing I've seen." As soon as he'd said it his memory took him back to the severed stump sticking out of the boot. He put the image of both back in a corner of his brain.

His eyes went down to the photograph from the hospital. The guy in the chair was wearing a hospital gown and socks. *DEA?* Cove thought, *it's drugs. Cutting the lips off of somebody flapping their mouth, but why a foot?*

The photograph came back into focus. The younger

man pushing the chair was wearing jeans, a long-sleeved western shirt and cowboy boots. The heels of the boots didn't have the acute angle of a Mexican heel, but he was almost too slender to be a Caucasian. A ball cap covered his face. Cove's eyes drifted to the belt buckle. It was not a silver rodeo buckle like the kind that most cowboys wore. It was a large leather-looking dark rectangle with a stitched ivory horse head. The buckle's border looked as if it was stitched with the same course white thread. The matching belt had a stitched floral design in the center with two overlapping "L" patterns stitched along the edges. The air in the room chilled.

Cove took a deep breath, let it out and looked at Mendiola. "Let me have a copy of this... I'll show it to a source."

"A source?" McGee asked.

Cove's eyes didn't leave Mendiola's, but they blinked. "Just somebody I know in the Hispanic community. Maybe he'll recognize the guy in the chair."

"Whoa. Let's slow this down," McGee said. "We don't want this out yet."

Mendiola looked at McGee. "We ain't got shit right now. What do we have to lose? I'll print another copy for him."

Chapter 6

Cove pulled out of the parking lot and turned left on 9th. At the junction of Main, he stopped and looked across the street at the old Chevron station. Other than one car parked in front of it, it looked dead. His blinker was off. He didn't know which direction he was going to turn. Looking down at the photograph, he studied the man pushing the wheelchair and again came to the same conclusion. After a moment, he pulled his phone out, opened up his contacts and found the number he was looking for. He selected it and it started to ring. Checking his rearview mirror, he listened to the phone. There was no one behind him and no traffic had passed on Main. After several rings, the call went to voice mail. He waited for the beep. "Charlie Cove. You around? Give me a call." Cove disconnected and stared at the phone. He wasn't sure he wanted to do this. What he wanted to do was figure out what had caused three fish to die in Morgan Creek.

He pulled onto Main and parked next to the curb. Bringing his phone back up, he dialed the number for the Salmon Fish and Game office and asked to speak to fish biologist Bob Johnson. Bob had pounded more creeks in Idaho studying fish than anyone Cove knew. He was in his sixties, had a balding head of white hair and a full white beard. His skin was red from years of sun. He was known to wear out a pair of wading boots each summer.

"Charlie, glad you called. George says you found some dead fish. What's going on?"

"I was wondering about whirling disease."

"They have crooked spines?"

"No, they looked healthy. In fact the one I opened up was full of nymphs."

"Then it's not whirling disease. It disfigures the spine and causes them to swim in circles. They can't feed. They usually die of malnutrition."

"What else could it be?

"Good question. Maybe hooking mortality."

"I looked for hook marks. There weren't any."

"If you find any more, I'll bet it's coming out of an old mine. You know of any old mines up there with springs coming out of them?"

"No, I don't. I've found plenty of old mines up here. I can't think of any that have water seeping out."

"Most of the rock up there is full of sulfides. There could be a spring in an old shaft that for some reason has developed an increased flow. That happens sometimes. I saw it on the South Fork at Yellowpine. The sulfides create sulfuric acid, and it leaches all sorts of heavy metals out like mercury. Even arsenic. I hope the hell that's not the case. We've been dealing with it in Blackbird Creek since I've been here. If this was late July or August and hotter than hell, I'd say it was oxygen levels, but it can't be. Can you do me a favor and see if any more turn up?"

"Yeah," Cove said, thinking about the message he'd just left and the photos with the lipless smile.

"If you find any more morts, collect them and get a hold of me. They've got to be fresh for the lab."

His phone beeped, and he saw it was Mendiola calling.

"Bob, I gotta take this call. I'll get back up there when I can." He clicked off.

"Yeah?"

"McGee's gone. What the hell was that all about with a Mexican informant?"

"Hispanic. I got a hunch I know somebody that knows something."

Mendiola paused. "You said he was a source in our Hispanic community. What's with that? A dozen Mexicans cutting hay here ain't exactly a community."

"I didn't say it was a he."

McGee's Jeep passed by, and Cove caught the man's face looking at him through the side mirror.

"There's eight ISP detectives in Idaho Falls," Cove said. "Seven of them are great. Why'd you end up with the one idiot?"

"I get why you can't stand McGee," Mendiola said. "He can be a fucking hemorrhoid. He tried to throw you under the bus. I get it. But he's gonna chase leads. He says––"

Cove interrupted, "McGee couldn't catch a cold." He hung up, rubbed his eyes and wondered why he'd allowed the detective to dig into his skin. Deep enough to hang up on Mendiola.

***

Juan Torres Rodriguez awoke, not realizing where he was for a long moment. His eyes focused and they caught the stare from Santa Muerte's skull. The candle had gone out and black wax had run down its side and puddled on the desk. Daylight came through the white drapes.

The edge of a dream stung him. He remembered that he was sitting in a chair, unrestrained and someone was cutting his ear off. His hand came up to the side of his head. The ear felt fine. He looked at the empty glass next to his saint and realized the mescal he'd poured was gone. He didn't recall drinking it and assumed his saint had accepted the offering. The dream disappeared like the flash from the muzzle of a gun, but its aura clung to him.

His body hurt. He got up, feeling as if he'd aged twenty years. After relieving himself in the toilet, he limped back to the window and peeked out through the side of the drapes. He was surprised to see the sun low in the west. He looked over at the clock and realized it was evening. He'd slept through the day.

From the black nylon bag, he pulled out an incense stick, studied it for a moment and then went into the bathroom where he retrieved a small bar of soap. Without pulling the wrapper off, he pushed the wood end of the stick into the flat of the soap, lit the stick and set it beside Santa Muerte with the soap acting as a base. The smoke coiled up around her effigy, and the grassy-licorice aroma of Aztec Copal touched each corner of the room.

He felt weak and took a long pull from the bottle of mescal. The liquid burned into his belly, and he felt a sudden flush of saliva in his mouth. After a few seconds, he struggled to the toilet, leaned over and vomited. Pain convulsed from his ribs and brought him to his knees. He whispered, "Santa Muerte, por favor..." After a few minutes he got up and made it back to the bed. He laid down for what he believed was a half hour, but when he opened his eyes, it was dark outside.

Rummaging around in the luggage, he found a cell phone and a small Ziploc bag of white pills. The letters OX were written in black ink on the baggie. He laid two pills in front of the Holy Saint of Death, recovered the pistol from under the pillow and dropped the loaded magazine into his palm. The smoke from the incense twisted towards the firearm. Flipping the empty glass over, he laid the two pills on its base and used the butt of the pistol magazine to beat them into course granules. He thumbed a 9mm cartridge from the magazine and used the base of it to grind the substance into a fine dust. When he was done, he pushed it into two fat lines. Taking a fifty dollar bill from the shoe box, he rolled it into a tube while watching the smoke twist around his goddess. Sticking the tube as far up his nose as he could get it, he leaned over and put the opening of the bill at the end of a line and violently snorted the powder.

It hit him like a hard slow-motion face slap, and he found himself twenty years younger in a hotel in Culiacán with his long-legged dark-haired compañera having the best night of his life. His troubles blew away like a warm summer wind.

Chapter 7

He looked at the clock on the dash. It was 2:54 p.m. Part of him wanted to talk to the guy he'd just left a message with, but a larger part of him regretted making the call. Cove didn't want to get the man involved. The fish were his priority. He needed to check Morgan Creek and make sure there weren't any more dead or dying fish. The badge on his shirt wanted to work Mendiola's case. It was like Jekyll and Hyde.

His phone buzzed, and he looked at the screen. It rang twice, and he felt his chest rise.

"Armando, how you doing?"

"Good, señor Cove, you?"

"Thanks for calling me back. I need to bounce something off you. Are you around your place right now?"

"About what?"

"Something you might be able to help with."

"I try, just ask."

"It's something I need to show you." Cove looked down at the photo and felt his pulse quicken. "I'll just swing by your place in forty-five if that'll work?"

58

For a moment Cove thought the call had been dropped.

Armando Barreras lowered his voice. "Not at the house. How 'bout up the draw across the road? Anderson Spring road a little ways?"

"Works for me." Cove said, and wondered why Barreras didn't want to meet at his home. There was something afoot. "See you in thirty, eh?"

He disconnected the call, dropped the truck's transmission into drive and pulled out onto Main. In the past, he'd given seized deer carcasses to the Barreras's. He'd chosen the family because they always seemed to be living on the edge. But he also knew that it might keep Armando from popping a closed-season deer. Now he wondered what the guy had something illegal hanging in his shed. If he'd shot a deer, there would be blood or hair in the bed of his truck. He'd have to figure out a way to take a look.

He liked the guy. Armando had helped him out by giving him the first break in the Terzi case. To a point, he thought he trusted him.

If he caught Barreras with a closed season deer, he wouldn't hesitate to seize it and write him a ticket. But it wasn't a case he'd like. He glanced back down at the photo. The more he looked at it, the more certain it was Barreras pushing the wheelchair. Cove started to doubt his assessment of the man. He didn't *think* that he was involved with drugs, but if he was connected to this guy, how could he not be?

On its face, Cove didn't believe that sneaking somebody out of a hospital was a crime. With that in mind, he believed he could maintain Armando as a confidential informant and not get him twisted into a charge of conspiracy or an accessory after the fact. However, if Armando had known 'Jose' was about to be arrested, that'd be a different issue, and he doubted he could protect him. Had it not been for the photo of the lipless smile–using Armando as an informant wouldn't bother him–but he felt like he was walking an unknown trail.

Cove turned off the Pahsimeroi road and up towards Anderson Spring. He could see fresh tire tracks in the dust. In less than a quarter of a mile, he came around a knob and found Armando's older Ford pickup facing him. Cove had no idea why this meeting had been orchestrated this way and it didn't smell right. Something was afoot, and he didn't have any sense what it could be. He unbuckled his seatbelt and stopped his truck with his door even with the Ford's tailgate. He stepped out and stole a glance into the bed of the truck. It looked like it'd been swept with a broom. He didn't see any blood. Barreras didn't get out of the pickup, and Cove caught him watching from his side mirror. Again, the lack of movement didn't feel right. Besides, he needed him out of the truck to get a look at his belt buckle.

Cove stuck his hand through the truck's open window and shook Barreras's hand. "Thanks for giving me a minute, Armando." The handshake felt too brief. Cove looked past him and saw a straw hat sitting on the passenger's seat but no ball cap. There was no way from this angle that he was going to get a look at the buckle.

"I heard you were using a cane," Armando said.

"I threw the damn thing in the dump."

Barreras looked towards the Pahsimeroi Road. "I need to get back soon."

Cove's head canted. "Everything okay with your family?"

"My littlest niño has earache."

"Your wife's down there though, eh?"

"Si, I just didn't want to complicate things." Barreras said it while rubbing his nose. "That's why I came here."

Cove had caught him covering his mouth, and he watched his eyes. They seemed to be flicking about, and his answer didn't feel right.

After an uncomfortable moment, Cove said, "Let me show you what I've got. Jump in my truck for a sec."

Cove hadn't seen Barreras for months, but he was confident the buckle in the photo was the same one he'd been wearing the last time the two had talked. It was distinctive. Cove's plan was to get a good look at the buckle. If it matched the photo, he was going to pull the picture out and confront him. If the buckle didn't look right or didn't match, he was going to roll with it and ask about the guy in the chair. If Barreras wasn't wearing the horse-head buckle, he wasn't sure what he was going to do.

Armando stepped out of his truck, exposing the back of his belt. It was dark leather with coarse white stitching that formed a continuous floral pattern on the belt. Cove managed to get inside his truck before Armando made it around to the passenger side. When he got in, Cove saw the buckle. He brought his hand up and rubbed his eyes and forehead.

For a second, he thought about dancing around it. Ease

into it. Maybe ask him about a trip to the hospital. Instead, he pulled the photograph out of a yellow legal pad.

He set the photo in Barrera's lap. "Who is he?"

Armando's face blanched. He stared at the photo without responding for perhaps thirty seconds. It just sat there on his thighs, untouched. Cove looked at the Mexican's hands. They were rough and calloused. The skin was cracked on the edges of his fingers. He thought he could see a hint of sweat forming on the man's skin.

"Look Armando, it's not illegal to move a guy out of a hospital... How do you know him?"

Armando shook his head. "Not me."

"No bullshit. That's you." Cove reached over and tapped the photo with his finger. "That's your buckle."

After a long pause, Barreras answered. "Lots of us have piteado belts."

"It's not just your buckle." Cove lowered his voice. "It's you, Armando."

"Señor Cove, **por favor,**" He met Cove's eyes. "Don't do this to me."

Cove studied him for a moment. His dark Latino skin had been razed by the sun and was set off by his coal-black hair. For a Mexican, he was tall. Maybe six-two. His thirty-five year old frame was skinny from agricultural work. "There's only two people who know you helped me with Terzi, and we're both in this truck."

"They'll kill my family first."

That caused Cove to pause. What little he knew about "Jose"–the severed foot and the fact he'd been using a lipless dead man's identity–gave the statement credibility. He was tempted to tell him to forget about it and go hug his bambinos.

"Why do you say that?" Cove asked. "What have you gotten sucked into?"

Armando looked out the windshield. "I got a call from Culiacán, it's en Sinaloa."

"Mexico?"

"Si. El hombre told me he had a friend that had been in a bad accidente' in Challis, and that I needed find him and check him in to a motel for three or four nights. He said he'd be in hospital. He didn't understand Challis didn't have a hospital. Took a while to find him."

"Who was the guy on the phone?"

"I have no idea, but they knew my wife's name, and that we have three little niños."

"They?"

"Narcos." Armando's hands came off his lap. "I couldn't say no."

"Why'd he call *you*?"

Armando looked at Cove and shook his head. His eyes were wide and glassy. "No idea. I know some of them were in the army. I served four years."

"Mexican army?" Cove asked.

"Si."

"He must have given you this guy's name."

"Señor Cove, if they find out, they will kill mi familia. They will make me watch. They'll do the same to you."

Cove's eyes blinked twice, and he bit his lip. "I haven't seen you for months. It'll stay that way. It'll never come back to you."

"Do you have a wife and kids?" Armando asked.

Cove shook his head. "No. Never married."

"Girlfriend?"

Cove studied the owl feather hanging from the mirror and wondered if he was putting Julie at risk once again. "Good question."

"I let Tomás run Harris's backhoe." Armando said. "He's my oldest. That's what he wants to do when he grows up."

Cove's phone buzzed, and he shut it off, annoyed with the interruption.

"Did they give you money for the room?"

"He was happy on the backhoe. I wish I could buy one."

For a moment Cove thought Armando meant that he'd been paid to move the man out of the hospital but dismissed it.

"Who paid for the room?'

Armando exhaled. "I used my money. His name is Marco. Marco Ayala. I got him a room at the Westbank. That's all I know."

Cove looked at the small calendar stuck to the glove compartment.

Armando looked at Cove. "Why are you involved in this? A game warden?"

Cove shook his head and exhaled. "Good question. Was that Monday? Five days ago?

"Si, Monday."

Cove swallowed. "You sure his last name wasn't Talavera?"

"Maybe. We have two last names. My full name is Armando Barreras Ortega. Ortega is my mother's name; Barreras is my father's. It's not my middle name, as you would call it. I was told to find Marco Ayala. I did what I was told. Talavera could be his other last name."

Armando studied Cove. His eyes didn't wander. Cove had never seen such a direct look from the man.

"Por favor, señor Cove. Do not take this as disrespect. Gringos look at me and mi famila. They see our run-down trailer sitting in the weeds." He looked at his feet. "Worn out botas." He looked back at Cove and gestured towards the Pahsimeroi. "But with mi familia, soy el mas rico de todos en la valle. Richer than a millionaire. I don't think gringos comprende."

The statement caused Cove to stop, and he stared at the mountains rimming the valley. They were covered in green grass with patches of black timber on their north facing slopes. A patch of snow clung to the rocks near the top of Mogg Mountain. *Does he think I'm white or Indian?* Cove looked down and found himself rubbing his thigh. Flicking his eyes back at Armando, he swallowed and gave a slight nod.

"What was he doing here?"

Armando Barreras shook his head. "No sé, nothing I want to know about. They say they are Cristianos, but they worship death."

***

He dialed the number from memory and listened to it ring five times.

"Bueno?"

"Es Juan Torres, señor."

There was a long pause before the man on the other side answered. "Confío en que recibió todo lo que necesitabas?"

"Si, everything was in the bag. Es muy bueno. Muchas gracious."

"Y usted va a ir a buscar la *other message? The object?*"

"I will get the other one. El hombre will get the message."

***

Cove drove down the Anderson Springs road. When he got to the Pahsimeroi road, he could see the Barreras place about two hundred yards up the valley and across the road. It was a faded singlewide trailer surrounded by dirt and a few weeds. Off to one side was a rough unpainted wooden shed with a corrugated metal roof. The shed's door was open and moved a bit with the breeze. It exposed a dark interior that looked empty. An older faded-red sedan was parked in front of the trailer. A tricycle and a bike lay beside it. A boy, who Cove guessed was ten, was chasing a younger kid around in a tight circle. Both had grins as big as the valley.

Cove turned down the road and pulled his phone out. The missed call had been from Julie. He called Mendiola.

"Your Jose is in the Westbank Motel in Idaho Falls. At least he was on Monday. He had three nights paid for."

"You're shittin' me," Mendiola exclaimed. "Who's your source?"

66

"She's nobody. A coyote in the sage."

"She hear this in a bar or what?"

"No, it's first-hand. It's good." Cove could almost see Mendiola chewing on this.

"Did she give a name?"

"He's using Marco Ayala."

"You just made my day. The judge was asking about the warrant this morning." Mendiola paused. "I'll give McGee's office a call and have them run down there and hit the place. Maybe he's still there."

"Let me know." Cove said.

"After the next election, you're going to be my first pick for chief deputy. I want you to think about it."

"Fred," Cove paused. "It'll be a cold day in hell when I wear a uniform with Custer's name on it. It'd be like a Jew wearing a swastika armband. Make sure your second choice knows what he's doing and doesn't have a problem working with a half-breed."

"Whatever." Fred's voice turned into a smile. "Charlie, about your source. You seeing some little chiquita you're not telling me about?"

Cove hung up.

***

The jibe brought Cove back to the call he'd gotten during the Barreras interview. He brought up his "Favorites" list on his phone and touched Julie Lake's number. He took a deep breath as he listened to the ringing. When he was just about to hang up, she answered.

"Hey warden, I was beginning to wonder."

"Yeah, it's been a while."

"How's Annie?"

"She misses you."

Julie paused, "I miss both of you. You weren't returning my calls. What's that about, Charlie?"

He pulled off the road and shut his truck off.

Cove answered with an exhale. "I think it's going to be a dry summer." He looked out the side window at the foothills on the other side of the river. "I wish it hadn't ended this way."

Julie's voice came up in pitch. "I didn't know it had."

He didn't answer for fifteen or twenty seconds. "We both have our demons."

"The same demon, Charlie." Her voice lowered in pitch. "I'd feel safer if they'd find his body. I thought it'd be better if I got a long way from Challis, but I still don't feel safe."

"They never found my father's body either."

"You never told me that."

"I didn't want you to believe that they might not find him. I figured a steelhead fisherman would snag him this spring. Sometimes bodies don't come up, though... Maybe low water. I don't know."

"I just want it to be like before."

Cove thought about the dream. His tongue found the sharp edge on his molar.

Julie asked, "How are the nightmares?"

Cove paused and wondered if she'd read his mind. "Same old reruns. You never talk of yours."

"I want my life back," Julie said. "I don't feel safe. Nights scare me... Are you still waking up at the same time?"

"Sometimes." Cove closed his eyes.

"How's your leg?"

He realized he was rubbing it. "Much better. My physical therapist had me throw the cane away. It was like a potlatch."

"I'm in the ladies room. I need to get back to my meeting. It's late, and they want to go home. I wish I felt the same way."

***

He pulled a cigarette out of the pack with his lips, brought the flame of the lighter to its tip and lit it. Sucking in deeply, he held the smoke for a moment and let it roll out his nose. He set the Marlboros on the dash and checked his mirror. Far behind him, he could see the taillights of a semi-truck in the growing darkness.

Pulling a business card from his pocket, he flipped it over and tried to read the scrawled phone number, but it was too dark. Bringing the card near the tip of his cigarette, he inhaled and illuminated the scrawl. The name Barreras was written below the number. With the cigarette still in his lips, he punched the number into his cell and brought it to his ear. As it rang, he took another hit on the cigarette.

A female voice answered. "Bueno?"

He took the Marlboro from his lips. "Estas Armando?
"Si, le hablo."

He brought the cigarette up and took another drag. There was some fumbling on the phone, and a male voice answered.

"Hello?"

"Ah mi amigo, soy yo, Marcos. Marcos Ayala." The smoke from his lungs clouded the phone. "I called to thank you for what you did for me."

There was a long pause. "You don't need to thank me, señor. We are paisanos. De nada."

"It's not nothing, te debo el dinero para el motel, y tambien para el gas."

"No, it was a favor. You owe me nothing, señor."

"I have a business proposition for you. Un trabajo."

Armando hesitated. "I already have a job. We are getting ready to cut alfalfa."

"This pays better, señor Barreras, much better. I'd like to meet your familia. We can go for a drive, and I'll tell you what you are going to do."

Armando Barreras's heart froze.

Juan Torres Rodriguez listened to the silence for a while and then hung up. He sat in the shadow of the Big Lost range and enjoyed his Marlboro. He was pleased. His message had been understood. He looked at the fading skyline to the west that seemed disjointed by the peaks and valleys and thought that someday he would take time off and run with the bulls of Pamplona. Feel their hot breath, and taste the stench of air filled with gore and testosterone. The smell of machismo. A set of headlights came over the hill. He closed his eyes and let the vehicle pass. Flicking the cigarette butt out the window, he thought about the face in his dream. The man that had been cutting his ear off. He'd known him for a few hours. He thought his name had been Carlos. It'd been a long time ago and it didn't matter because Carlos, or whatever his name had been, was the one who had been in the chair.

Chapter 8

Cove turned left on the highway, paralleling the Salmon River. There were a few tourists on the road. They drove motor homes and pulled fifth-wheel campers and seemed to be in a rush. He tried to glimpse the river through the cottonwoods out of his side window. Crossing over Bruno's Bridge, he had a hard time keeping from rubbernecking into the river, looking for Terzi's body. It needed to be buried in a hole.

He turned up Morgan Creek. When he got to the place where he'd found the dead fish, he pulled his truck into the same spot the Escalade had been parked. He dumped his duty belt behind the seat, stripped down to his t-shirt, changed from his green Levi's into a pair of black nylon shorts and put on a pair of felt-soled wading boots. Dropping the tailgate, he let Annie out. He went over the fence; Annie followed and went under it. The game trail had fresh heart-shaped elk tracks covering the older boot prints. A calf had been the last to use the trail through the willows. The woody smell of the jungle enveloped him.

When he got to the creek, a pair of mallard ducks jumped up and flew off with loud rasping calls. Annie quivered but held at his side.

Cove looked into the clear water and was relieved to not see any dead fish. He assumed a mink had found the three that he'd left. Annie looked at him as if she were asking a question. He moved his hand toward the water, and said, "Okay." Annie slipped into the creek like a big brown otter and turned around at mid-current. When her feet touched the bottom, she lapped water.

He walked over to the clump of willows where he'd found the stashed fishing rod and made sure the long grass didn't conceal a bleach jug that he'd missed. He moved up the creek and found a beaver dam that formed another pool. Stepping up, he saw a foot-long fish dart into the shadows. There were several light yellow beaver cuttings in the bottom of the pool but no belly-up fish. He fought the brush along the creek for a hundred yards without finding anything of interest other than the rusty tines of an old pitchfork that had been there long enough for the wooden shaft to have rotted off.

When he got back down to the beaver dam, he was thinking the three dead fish would remain a mystery. The guttural squawk of a great blue heron, a hundred yards up the West Fork, woke him to the fact that its water *could be* the source of whatever had killed the fish. He crossed over the beaver dam. Forty yards up the side creek, he found a dead fish. He stepped into the cold water, and Annie followed him. Glancing at her, he wondered if the two of them should be wading in it. He pulled the fish out. It was an 8" long cutthroat trout with a slight covering of white fungus. The black pupils had turned white, and they made Cove flash back to the dream and Terzi's ice-white eyes.

He was good at estimating how long deer and other

animals had been dead by using temperature, degree of bloat, dehydration and insect activity. But his knowledge about what happened after a fish died and sat in cold water was lacking. Certainly the temperature would slow deterioration. He guessed that this fish had been dead a couple of days, and he regretted not walking up the side creek the day he'd found the original three. Other than the fungus and the white pupils, the fish looked okay. He'd put a large Ziploc in his back pocket in case he'd found dead fish but recalled Bob Johnson saying they needed to be fresh. He decided this one was too far gone. He slid the fish back into the water and stepped out onto the bank. He motioned for Annie to do the same by bringing his palm to his thigh. He felt the scar on his thigh, looked down and rubbed his finger across it. It was a round divot about a half-inch wide that was perfectly centered in his leg. He hadn't thought about it before, but the sight of it–so perfectly centered–made him wonder what the outcome of the fight would have been if the bullet had missed his femur and hadn't crippled him. Terzi had gotten lucky, and he'd been jinxed. It'd been like the flip of a coin.

A harsh "keee-ahrrr" from the sky brought his head up. It was a red-tail, drifting with the currents in the blue sky. The hawk floated up the drainage and disappeared.

He looked up the drainage. The bottom of the West Fork, where Cove and Annie were, was a smaller version of the heavily willowed main fork. There was a Forest Service road that came off the Morgan Creek road about a quarter of a mile from where his truck was parked. It crossed a bridge and followed along the bottom of the West Fork drainage. He could see the junction of a second road that

74

crossed the creek and climbed up a ridge on the creek's south flank. The slope of this ridge faced north, and was timbered with fir trees. The south facing side of the drainage was baked by the sun and was vegetated with grasses and scattered sage.

The road that followed along the West Fork went for about five miles and then turned to the right at Blowfly Creek. At the confluence of the side creek, six miles of horse trail led to the source of the West Fork where three small mountain lakes sat in a glacial cirque. There were several smaller creeks that flowed into the West Fork from the south. The first one was Fourth Spring Creek and the last was the East Fork. The East Fork was the only one with a road in the bottom. It was a washboard of a trail that followed the gut of the creek for a mile or so before it zigzagged up a steep spur ridge.

It was wild country that a person could get lost in.

***

Annie jumped in the back of the truck without any urging from Cove. He retrieved the keys from under the rock where he'd hidden them, got in and drove up to the West Fork road and crossed over Morgan Creek. He paused at the bridge and checked the water, half expecting to see another dead fish. Seeing nothing that caught his eye, he continued up the West Fork. He stopped at the junction that split off and headed to the head of Fourth Spring Creek. He got out and walked to the bridge, studying the dark pool below it. Two dead fish stopped his gaze. He waded in and confirmed that they were covered with about the same amount of white fungus as the fish below. As he turned, he noticed a large bird carcass rotting just under the surface. Most of its feathers had come loose, making it look like a strange lizard-like creature. He studied its narrow bill. It was about three inches long and almost black. The upper bill had large nostrils and fine teeth along the edge that mated with the slender bottom bill. The top bill had a bit of a hook at the end that rolled over the bottom bill. He recognized it. The dead bird was a merganser–a duck that lived by eating fish.

Cove climbed out of the creek, wondering how smart it was to expose his skin to the water. The one case he'd worked where someone had dumped something toxic into the river, the kids had complained of a burning. For the moment, his skin felt fine. He was beginning to believe the point that the biologist had raised about mining activity was on the money.

He got out of his wet shorts, put his uniform on and snugged his duty belt to his hips. He looked up the drainage. The sun was well into the late afternoon and was shining from the west. From where he was, the roadbed shaded the creek bottom, but from about the midpoint of the channel to the far side, the sun penetrated the clear water and illuminated the rocks along its bottom. It looked clean and healthy.

Above him, the creek braided back and forth through head-high willows and tall cottonwoods. He continued idling up the road, looking into the creek when the vegetation allowed. He found one dead fish and another merganser. They were all in the same condition. No fresh carcasses. He came up with two theories; either a one-time chemical slug had run down the drainage and poisoned the fish and birds, or it was still coming down the creek. He thought about the two theories. If it'd been a one-time poisoning, he assumed it was from somebody who had driven up and dumped something into creek. It had happened during his first summer as an Idaho warden. Somebody had dumped an unknown substance upriver at the small town of Clayton. He'd gotten the tip from a mother who was concerned about her kids swimming in the Salmon River. Whatever it was had killed several fish and given the kids a rash. He'd contacted several potential witnesses in the little mining town, but nobody stepped forward. He was so new to the game that he didn't even know what law had been broken. In the end, it didn't matter, since the residents seemed to believe that keeping their lips zipped was more important than having clean water.

Thinking about his one-time dump theory, Cove continued up the drainage, looking for tracks in the dust that would indicate that somebody had pulled over. At the same time, he studied the creek whenever there was a break in the willows.

For the most part, the road stayed in the sagebrush just above the riparian vegetation that the creek wandered through. There were several places where somebody could have disposed of a liquid into the creek, but for the most part the road stayed too far from the water to make it practical. At each possible dump spot, Cove slowed down and stuck his head out the window while studying the dust. When he got to the confluence of the East Fork, he got out on the bridge and studied the water. It was clear and moss-free. He examined the wood timbers along the edges of the bridge. There were no dents, or transfer paint from a barrel, or some other indication that something had been dumped in the creek. He decided that the one-time dump of a toxic substance probably hadn't happened.

He drove up the East Fork. About three-quarters of a mile up, he found where somebody had taken a bulldozer and scarred the hillside, presumably using the blade to expose the geology of the area in what he'd heard referred to as "exploratory mining." The land was doing its best to reclaim the miner's effort. The cut was covered by sagebrush and bunch grasses. He could not see where any serious mining–such as a shaft–had been attempted, but it told him that somebody, years ago, had thought that the drainage held hidden wealth. There had to be an old mine shaft somewhere that was killing the drainage. He turned around. When he hit the West Fork, he turned left and followed it to Blowfly Creek. At the confluence, he got out and walked the creek. He found nothing out of the ordinary; no dead critters.

He turned around and drove down the drainage to the bridge where he'd found the first merganser. He started up the road that led to the head of Fourth Spring Creek. It gave him a good view of the valley, the confluence of the West Fork and up the Pahsimeroi. A flash of light came from across Morgan Creek. He stopped and looked. There was a vehicle parked on the road. It looked like McGee's. He shut his engine off and grabbed his binoculars. It was a dark blue Durango–not McGee's Jeep. He could see someone in the driver's seat. The flash came again, but this time through the ten-power binoculars, he realized there was a guy in the driver's seat staring back at him with a pair of binoculars. Cove's hair came up, and for a moment the two studied each other, and then the SUV continued up Morgan Creek.

Cove thought about what had just happened. The guy had done exactly what he'd done. In a sense, it was a normal thing to do in this remote country. If it'd been a rancher who was grazing cows on the forest, he'd want to know who was up poking around. There were some poachers who preferred beef over venison. However, ranchers drove pickup trucks, not SUVs. It could be the person he'd gotten the tip on. The guy who he suspected was using road kill deer for bear bait up on Morgan Summit. But that theory didn't wash, since someone hauling bait would probably be driving a pickup truck too.

He stepped out of the truck, took his phone out, saw that it had service and called the Fish and Game office in Salmon. He brought it to his ear and watched the SUV disappear up the valley.

***

Cove called Fisheries Biologist Bob Johnson at his office in Salmon and briefed him about finding additional fish. Cove told him that one was a cutthroat.

"With both cutthroat and rainbows," Johnson explained, "I can't believe it's disease. It's gotta be something in the water. It almost has to be from a mine."

He explained that if Cove found any seepage with a yellow or orange tint to it that he should look for a mine above it.

When Cove told Johnson about the mergansers, the guy paused for a moment. He wasn't sure that if a scavenger ate fish poisoned by mine waste–such as arsenic–that it too would be poisoned but thought it possible. What he *was* sure of was that anything exposed to water with high levels of arsenic would die. Hearing that, it made Cove wonder why he'd gotten in the creek and allowed Annie to join him. He felt stupid.

"Look," Johnson said, "get a water sample. I'll send a tech your way to pick it up. I'll get it off to the lab and we'll see if it's got arsenic in it."

***

Cove found himself gloving-up to take the water sample. Having no other clean container, he used a one-gallon Ziploc bag for the sample. He drove down Morgan Creek, turned north on the highway and followed the Salmon River to the confluence of Pahsimeroi. The trip had taken him a half hour. He parked his truck facing the highway so that Johnson's tech would not fail to see the shield on the side of his truck and miss him.

While Cove was waiting, Mendiola called.

"McGee's crew hit the Westbank. He flew the coop. Been gone for two days. But it was him. The description fits. Maid found a cervical collar under the bed. She'd put it in lost and found. They ran it down to the lab and are pulling prints right now. McGee said the blue UV light showed all sorts of good latents. Some are gonna be the maid's, but our guy's prints have to be there too. It's been moved to the head of the pile, and the lab will run anything they get through AFIS tonight. I'm betting we get a hit. This fuckwad has to have a record."

"Glad somebody's cases get priority down there," Cove said. "I've gotta dead creek."

For a moment the conversation came to a halt, and then Mendiola went on. "If McGee comes up with leads to chase, let's run down there."

"No," Cove said. "Not gonna happen. I'm on George's shit list as it is."

"I'll call him. He owes me."

Cove wondered what favor Mendiola was referring to. *Was it over Terzi?* For a moment, he was tempted to stick the sheriff up and ask him what he was talking about, but he kept his mouth shut.

"I gotta close this one," Mendiola said. "I can't spend the rest of my days wondering who the fuck got his foot sawed off. Got enough shit in my closet."

"Look," Cove said, "The guy's gone. Phoenix or a beach in Baja. If the body's here, some hunter'll find it. They come up with prints you can get a warrant for him. Sooner or later, somebody'll hook him up."

"If they come up with a lead," Mendiola said, "I'm gonna head down to Idaho Falls."

"Good, take Jenks."

"He says he's gluten intolerant."

Cove noticed a blue SUV approaching from the south with an out-of-state license plate. It was on the highway coming from the opposite direction from where the tech would be coming. It was dusty. It looked like the vehicle that had glassed him from the Morgan Creek road.

Cove studied the rig. It was a blue Dodge Durango. "What the hell's gluten got to do with anything?"

As the rig approached, the vehicle slowed and signaled to turn up the Pahsimeroi. Cove studied the driver through the passenger's window. It was too dark to catch the man's face, but his behavior troubled Cove. The driver hadn't turned to look at him. A game warden–or for that matter any law enforcement officer–parked by the road in this remote country was a magnet for eyeballs. It was as if the man wanted to be invisible, and it went back to Cove's theory that it'd been the same rig that had stopped and studied him from Morgan Creek.

"I need food when I'm chasing somebody," Mendiola answered.

When the SUV turned up the Pahsimeroi, Cove turned and looked through his back window, trying to catch the rear plate, but Annie's dog box blocked his view.

On the highway to the north, Cove saw a truck signaling to turn. It had a government license plate.

"I gotta hand over a water sample."

"What are you talking about?" Mendiola asked. "How 'bout we powwow for dinner?"

***

When Rodriguez had passed the cop in the pickup truck, he opened the console on the seat and pulled out the 9mm Beretta, stuck it under his leg and checked his mirror. He'd done three years in a federal prison for conspiracy for trafficking in methamphetamine. At his sentencing, the judge had made it clear that if were caught in the U.S. after his release, he'd do another seven. It wasn't going to happen. He'd shoot the Indian cop in the face, pull the memory card from his dash cam, shoot him in the head again and drive off and change to his other vehicle plates. It'd be easy. He would have done the same thing the night of the wreck, but he'd already ditched the gun.

When the singlewide came into view, he pulled over and studied it. The trailer faced the county road. A sunbaked red car was parked near the front door. He could see two Hispanic kids riding bikes on the dirt road in front of the trailer. They looked like they were racing. There was no sign of Barreras's pickup truck. He checked his mirror and brought a pair of binoculars up to his face. A small child was playing in the dirt in the shade of the house. He studied the windows but didn't see any movement.

Pulling a Vick's vapor inhaler from his shirt pocket, he unscrewed the lid, brought it to his nose and drew the fumes into each of his nostrils. He laid his head back on the seat and let his sinuses clear while studying his mirror. If the cop had turned to follow him, he would have been here by now.

Grabbing his stainless coffee mug, he unscrewed its base and fished out a jeweler's Ziploc from inside. It held a tablespoon of white powder. He set it on the Durango's console. Pulling a large folding knife out of his pant pocket, he stuck his thumb on the side of the blade and pushed it open, exposing a serrated edge. Sticking the blade into the powder, he removed a housefly-sized scoop. Pinching off one side of his nose, he put the knife's tip into his nostril and inhaled the coke. His eyes slammed open. Taking another scoop, he did the other nostril and felt his body come alive. Not quite there, he took two more snorts and felt his Aztec blood boom through his veins. He felt like a bull in the ring that had never seen a man on foot but now had one in front of him. He was *toro bravo*. A big black machismo bull.

Wiping his nose, he dropped the Durango into gear, drove to where the boys were playing and rolled down his window.

"Hola, mis amigos. ¿Dónde está tu padre?"

The tallest boy pointed up the road. "Él está trabajando. He's at work."

Rodriguez nodded. "¿Cómo te llamas?"

The boy smiled and looked down. "Tomás."

Rodriguez retrieved a small pocketknife from the dashboard and held it out to the boy. "Hombre needs a knife."

The boy's face lit up, flashed his pearl-white teeth and accepted the gift.

Rodriguez looked at the slender Latina woman staring from the porch and grinned. She had long black hair framing her high cheeks and strong jaw. He turned to the boy, "I'll see you later, mi amigo."

He drove up the Pahsimeroi and noticed a line of dust coming toward him. As the vehicle got closer, he recognized the blue and white Ford from his hospital escape, and he stuck his hand out and flagged the driver down.

"Señor Barreras, mi amigo!"

For a moment, Armando didn't reply. His mouth felt stuck.

"Señor Ayala?"

"Ayala is dead. Call me Juan." Rodriguez canted his head. "Get in." The Hispanic spoke with an edge as if his so-called amigo had a choice.

Armando hesitated and then got out of his truck, walked around to the rear of the Durango and got in the side door. Rodriguez put the SUV into drive and started up the road, leaving the Ford idling.

Armando turned to the driver and spoke in Spanish. "Where are you taking me?"

Rodriguez brought a pack of Marlboros to his mouth, took one in his lips and lit it. He didn't offer one to Armando.

For perhaps a mile, Rodriguez smoked his cigarette and acted as if he were the only one in the vehicle. Finally he flipped the butt out the window and spoke in Spanish. "I find your wife very attractive." He dipped his head. "She is worth a small fortune in Tijuana. Americans love Mexican pussy."

Armando stared through the windshield and brought his fist to his mouth. He was unable to breath.

After a while, Rodriguez continued in Spanish. "You're perfect for this job. I pay well, and it's not hard work. When it's done, you can play soccer with your boys or whatever the fuck you do up here." Rodriguez brought the truck to a stop, and leaned towards Armando, smiling like a snake. "I can get more for Tomás than for your wife."

***

Mendiola was sitting at the table drinking coffee. His face seemed to have more creases in it.

Cove sat down across from him. "Expecting a long night?"

"Decaf. McGee's got a theory."

Cove's lips turned up. "About Bigfoot?"

"I kinda miss those guys. Wandering around at night, playing their Sasquatch calls and getting lost," Mendiola said. "But no, he says you know too much."

Cove nodded. "He's getting smarter."

Cove turned to the approaching waitress. With the braces and pigtails, she looked like she was fourteen. "Just a hamburger and fries. Hold the onions." He turned to Mendiola. "You order?"

"Yep." When the waitress was gone, Mendiola continued. "Seriously, he says you know too much about the case. Brought up the chainsaw again, and the fact you knew where Jose was hanging out, but says you waited to tell us until he was gone." His eyes narrowed. "Says it's too coincidental."

Cove gave a half snort, took a swallow of water and looked out the window at a cow dog sleeping in the shade next to a beat up pickup.

"He doesn't think you've got a source." Mendiola said. "He's insisting you produce your informant."

"He can piss up a rope." Cove eyed Mendiola for a moment. "I don't think I told you this, but Jose's tied in with the cartels. That stays here."

"My kid wants you to hunt deer with us this fall."

"He expecting trouble?" Cove's eyes twinkled. "Wondering who's filling his mom's tag?"

The waitress slid three plates in front of them and smiled, showing her braces. "Holler if you need something else."

Cove looked at the two dishes in front of Mendiola. One looked like sliced roast beef or maybe lamb with mashed potatoes, and the smaller dish had four light-colored lumps that resembled chicken but wasn't.

Mendiola saw where Cove was looking. "Grab one." Mendiola picked a lump up with his fingers and sucked whatever it was into his mouth, chewed for a moment and set part of it back on the plate. "Your informant know that for sure? The cartels?"

Cove swallowed a French fry. "Your kid go through hunter education yet?"

"He's signed up for August." Mendiola studied Cove. "You said your informant got it first hand?"

"What are those things?" Cove asked looking at the plate. "He did. I need to figure out what's killing everything in the West Fork."

"Did you say, '*he*'?"

Cove shook his head, looked over at the dog and swallowed. The dog hadn't moved. "No, '*she*'."

Mendiola set whatever he was eating back on his plate and studied him for a moment. "I'm trying to think this through. A guy sneaks a buddy out the hospital, and your source claims she was there–more or less. Was she the driver? How the hell does she fit into this?"

"The cervical collar. Doesn't that confirm her? Isn't that the bottom line?"

"Just askin'."

Cove frowned. "Leave it alone. McGee can piss up a rope."

"My kid thinks you're gonna teach him how to track an ant across a rock."

Cove looked at Mendiola. "My source is off limits."

"I'm starting to get that idea. Not a cat I'm gonna poke. The other thing he brought up was wanting to know who all knows about the photo you flashed around." Mendiola picked up his coffee mug, took a drink and set it down. "I'm assuming you showed it to her and nobody else?"

"Let me get this straight." Cove's eyes narrowed. "McGee doesn't think I've got an informant, and he's worried that this person–that doesn't exist–is gonna blab about the photo? I'm confused."

"He's talked about both."

"He's a schizophrenic idiot. Call up his boss, and get somebody worth a shit up here. They've got some good guys in that shop." Cove shook his head, and his staccato voice took over. "I said I was going to show the photo to a source. It's how I got her to rollover. Now... why the shit I volunteered to do it is a mystery."

"Is she gonna keep her mouth shut?"

"If she doesn't, you'll have another lipless photo in your file." Cove looked back down at Mendiola's side dish. "What the hell is that stuff?"

"Pig's feet." He glanced towards the kitchen. "Martha makes 'em up for me."

Cove stared at the plate and grimaced. "You've *got* to be kidding me."

"You sound like my wife. She won't let me eat 'em at home. Old Basque dish." He slid the plate towards Cove. "Try one. They're damn good."

Chapter 9

Cove looked at the owl feather on the mirror for a moment and glanced at the small calendar on his glove box. The flavor of the salt and grease from the French fries was still stuck to his tongue. He'd circled today's date. June 21st. The solstice. He turned and headed towards his house. He could kill two birds with one trip.

He opened a five-gallon plastic bucket in his garage and served up two scoops of dog food in Annie's green dish. Grabbing an internal-framed backpack off the wall, he brought it inside and threw together a light camp outfit that consisted of a thin foam pad, a summer-weight sleeping bag and a baggie full of dried elk meat. From a shelf in his closet, he retrieved the battered cardboard box that his grandfather had given him and slipped it into the pack.

Annie jumped in the bed of the truck, and the two headed down the county road back towards Challis. The little town had about zero traffic. A few pickup trucks moved. He saw prosecutor Mike Pallid step out of his office and act as if he hadn't seen Cove. At the junction of the highway, he turned and saw the Cat's Ears sticking up several miles to the north. The twin-towered butte was unremarkable, other than the locals said its profile mimicked the top of a cat's head. The two ears were made of short jumbles of pale rock, and its scalp was covered by darker brush. Cove thought the ears looked more like the short tufts of a screech owl than those of a cat's.

Cove's phone vibrated. He looked at the screen and discovered that it was a text from Julie.

"Call me, please. I just got a tip I need to confirm."

Cove gazed at the message. She wanted *to use him* as a news source. After a mile or so on the highway he pulled over and called her and brought the phone to his good ear.

"Hey warden, thanks for calling me right back." Julie said enthusiastically.

"What's this tip?"

"Is a good mystery the only way I can get you to call me? What have you and Annie been doing?"

He told her about the West Fork die-off and explained that the current belief from the biologist was that it was runoff from an old mine.

"That's huge. Is EPA involved?"

"No, I'm the only one working on it right now. I haven't told the Forest Service about it yet, but it's on their ground. Our biologists are waiting on a water sample I sent in. I'm planning on pounding the drainage in the morning. Annie and I are going to camp up there tonight."

"We never camped."

"We'll be on top of the Cat's Ear. C'mon up."

"Cat's Ear?

"You could be here by midnight. I've got a delicious bag of jerky for breakfast."

"That place even on a map?"

Cove regretted bringing up his plans. "What's this about a tip?"

"I got a call from a source in Challis. She said the sheriff's office had found a severed foot. She said you were there. Is that true?"

"About the foot or me?"

"Both, wise-guy."

Cove looked down at the river below the highway. It was flanked by bands of tall cottonwoods. The bark on the trees looked like wrinkled elephant hide. None of the trunks were straight. The trees looked jumbled and confused. They'd angle off in one direction and bend back the other way. Several of them had two trunks forming a rough V shape. Their leaves were stiff, the color of dark jade and they held firm in the wind. The breeze had stripped a few catkins from the trees, and they looked like lost puffs of floating goose down.

"If you run this, Fred'll know where it came from before he gets done with the first paragraph."

"I take that to mean you were there?"

"Julie––"

"She said it's all over town. Some guy from California had a bad wreck, and it was in his truck."

After a moment he relaxed. He knew she wasn't going to throw him under the bus. "Wrong state. It's Jenks's case, but if you call him, he'll tell you more than he's supposed to. Just call Fred. He might talk to you."

"I talked to your mom."

"Call him. And tell him I wouldn't talk to you."

"He already thinks that."

Cove looked down a the river twisting through the cottonwoods. A heron stood on the far edge and stared into an eddy.

"Give him a call."

After she'd hung up, he thought about the call. *Did she need a source or was it an excuse?*

Once in Morgan Creek, he took a right turn onto a smaller rocky road that switchbacked up a spur ridge and paralleled a tiny creek called Gooseberry. Except for the vegetation down in the creek, the ridges and draws were covered with sagebrush that was as crinkled as an old woman and interspersed with bunch grass that still had a bit of green in it.

When he hit the main ridge, Cove stopped for a moment and studied the terrain. He turned off his cell phone and put it in the console. He reached over and turned off the radio. The last thing he wanted was George or Fred or somebody else asking where he was. Although he was still in his patrol area, he was not on state business.

The country was treeless. It drained to the south into the Salmon River. It was steep. Either down or up, with nothing in between. He turned right on the ridge top, and the road quickly degenerated into a two-track that had been made by decades of truck traffic bouncing through the brush.

The Cat's Ears came into view, capped by a cloudless blue sky. It was made of what geologists called the Challis volcanics. They claimed the formation was at least forty million years old. Cove's ancestors would have said that it was older than memory. Both were probably right.

He parked at the end of the two-track, dropped the tailgate and said, "Okay." Annie jumped out. He took his duty belt off, set the heavy rig behind the seat of his truck, stripped off his uniform shirt and set it over the weapon. Locking the truck, he shouldered the backpack over his t-shirt, cinched the waist belt and cut up the hill. The pack was lightweight and felt good on his back.

After a few minutes, he found the old trail. It looked like a game trail, but most of those seemed to never have a beginning or an end. They'd start off as a well-travelled path and after a hundred yards or so, they'd fizzle out. This trail seemed to have a purpose. It started at an obscure spot at the bottom of the butte and led to the top of the pile of rock that formed the first of the two ears. It never quit until the top. Cove believed the trail was manmade. Not scratched out with a tool, but made by repeated trips. Either by miners from a different generation, or by people that no longer lived in this country. Perhaps both had used it, but he'd never found any indication of mining on the butte. Two years previous, he'd found the trail after getting a tip about an illegal sheep hunt that had taken place on the ridge.

The trail was steep. Cove slowed his pace and locked his knees with each step. At first his thigh ached, but after two hundred yards, it seemed to loosen up. Annie followed behind him. He was breathing through his mouth, and it brought the taste of the oily sage and dry dust kicked up by his boots to his tongue. Near the top, the trail cut through large boulders and a few greenish-gray mountain mahogany bushes that were the size of small fruit trees, but mimicked the twisted sagebrush. Sweat trickled down the sides of his face. Annie's tongue hung from her mouth. After climbing non-stop for an hour, the two made it just short of the top. He dropped the pack, pulled out a water bottle, filled his cupped hand and let her drink. After two handfuls, he put the bottle in the pack and felt the dryness in his own mouth.

He examined the large rock that stood before him. It was bigger than his truck and had a flat surface that leaned out, sheltering its base. The top half of the rock was covered in orange and yellow lichens. Reaching out, he placed his palm on the course surface and felt the heat left by the late afternoon sun. The bottom of the monolith was blackened, and the soil along the edge was sooty from long-ago campfires. He walked around the rock and located a figurine painted under an angle of jutting stone. The stick figure was dark red on a spot that was devoid of lichens. It was about six inches high, had the two legs and arms of a man, but its head had two points sticking out as if it had horns and was part beast. Above the human figure was a half circle that had straight lines that fanned out. It was made using the same red pigment. There was no doubt in Cove's mind that the second symbol was a rising or setting sun. But he had no idea what the shape of the man's horned head meant, nor did he understand the implication of these two pictographs that were drawn by a forgotten man high up on this butte. He squatted down and studied the black soil. He found three tiny obsidian flakes and part of a mussel shell. It was an odd place to camp and cook. It was a day's walk to the river where the shell had come from and still much farther to the nearest source of obsidian.

Cove walked the few feet to the top of the ear. Looking west, he judged he had about an hour of sunlight. To the southeast, he could see beyond the butte's other ear and up the Pahsimeroi drainage with the parallel ridges of the Lemhi and Lost River mountains walling the sides of the valley. To the north, he could see where the Salmon River canyoned through a wall of rock. To the south, terrain hid the bottom of Morgan Creek, but the drainage slashed a line through the hills from the river up to the high country and bordered the roadless wilderness to the west.

He looked on the ground and relocated the light-green stone among the indigenous clay-colored rocks. Squatting down, he picked it up. It was a flat crescent shape about three and a half inches in length with long parallel flakes coming from the edges. He'd found the tool, along with the pictographs, while working the sheep case. He didn't believe a long-ago hunter had lost it. It was his belief that this place–this knob on a two-eared butte–had at some point in time possessed an untellable significance, and the tool had been placed here many, many generations ago for a reason.

He sat down on a stump-high rock with the stone knife, and rubbed his thumb across the flat surfaces, feeling where the flakes had been broken off by pressure from the tip of an antler. He felt its edge while looking into the distance. It wasn't as sharp as it'd been when its maker had formed it from the parent stone. The winds of time had abraded it. Cove considered this and wondered how many summer breezes had blown over this butte before its lithic edge was dulled.

He could see no roads. No buildings. No farmer's fields or power lines. No sign of man, other than the stone knife he held and the clothes he wore. The view hadn't changed since his last visit. It hadn't changed in hundreds, or more likely, thousands of years.

***

Still sitting on the rock, Cove pulled off his t-shirt and faced the setting sun. The orange rays met his almond-colored skin and made his chest glow like a candle in a paper bag. He unlaced his boots, set them aside and took off his socks. The bare soles of his feet palmed the earth.

Unstrapping his watch, he pushed it into his pant pocket. He picked the green stone knife back up and watched the shadows fill the draws. Warm air came up the butte and licked his hair. He was about to embark on a journey he knew nothing about.

While he was growing up, the white kids had called him rez-boy and blanket-ass. Tribal kids had called him half-breed. He'd wanted to be done with it and be white. And now he found himself on a rocky knob at 7,000 feet, feeling ignorant. He thought about the reflection of himself that he'd seen in the river. It'd been empty, his edge abraded like the stone knife he held in his hand.

It had started right there beside the river. Inside Terzi's trailer. Since then, his nightmares had been so vivid that some nights he didn't dare sleep. If he'd nod off, the feeling of the first bullet slamming his chest would shock him awake. Sometimes it was the second bullet taking his leg out or feeling his blood forming a warm pool around his dying body. Each dream was bolder than the memory of that day. Several times he'd snapped awake terrified but with no remembrance of a dream.

He watched as the sun touched the horizon. Its shape flowed oddly outwards. It was no longer a round orb but a flowing mass without form, its heat melting and disappearing into the earth. There seemed to be an indefinable pause. A long moment of calm that couldn't be measured with a clock. It was if the earth quit breathing. There was no noise. Nothing moved. The light didn't change. Everything just hung. And then it was done. The breeze turned and came flowing down from the higher country enveloping Cove's body. He breathed it in and realized that for a while, his chest had mimicked the earth's interlude.

He slipped his feet into his boots, dropped off the top, retrieved his pack and returned to the rock. Again his boots came off. He pulled the box out of the pack and untied the leather thong. The last time he'd looked at the contents was when his grandfather was walking away from him.

There were three items in the box. The largest was the coal-black wing of a raven. It was a foot in length. Had it not been dried, it would have doubled in size. On its trailing edge, it had eighteen long black primary feathers. The shaft of each was set off-center, with innumerable barbs flowing off each side and locking together, forming a stiff lightweight surface that was as thin and smooth as sheet metal but as light as the air. Each feather overlapped the next. On top of the primaries lay eighteen secondary feathers. They were much shorter and softer. It was an incredible opus that no human could duplicate. Its function was to move the wind of the earth.

The next item was a cylinder of dried silver-sage colored plant stems with long slender leaves. It was somewhat like a cigar, except the individual plants were laid out in the same direction and were held together with wraps of brown thread. Cove brought it to his nostrils and breathed in the aroma of the white sage. Its smell had a much more sugared flavor than the course brush around him.

The last item resembled a long braid of blonde hair cut from a woman. It was the hair of mother earth; sweetgrass. The ends were tied with the same brown thread. Without being told, he knew his grandmother had been the one who had harvested it and braided it. He had no idea how old it was, but she had been dead for over twenty years.

Towards Gooseberry Creek, a great horned owl called, "who-hoo-hoo-oo." Cove smelled the two bundles and looked to the north towards the river canyon that was disappearing in the darkness. He didn't know why, but he chose the sage. He put the sweetgrass back in the box and then paused, feeling a panic. Recalling the lighter in the pack, he relaxed and dug it out. He'd never done this before. He thought he'd seen his father doing it once, but it may have been a dream.

He put the flame of the lighter to one end of the dried sage and blew on it until it flamed up. When his breath died the flame went out, but the end glowed like the orange orb of the sun before setting. An earthy-sweet smoke poured out of the clump.

Next to Cove's foot was a flat rock camouflaged by lichens. He picked it up and realized it was a piece of porous lava unlike the other igneous rocks that formed the peak. In one sense, it didn't belong here but in another sense, it did. It had been tumbled in a stream, and someone had carried it to the top of this point. He scooted his butt off the rock he'd been sitting on, placed the lava rock between his legs and put the smoking sage on it. Leaning forward, he picked up the jet-black raven wing and began fanning the warm smoke around him.

Annie's ears came up. Her head canted and she studied Cove. She watched the beating of the raven's wing bring life to the pungent smoke. It moved like a chimera flowing in rippling coils around her champion, twisting and morphing.

Cove felt the smoke washing over his pores like steam from a shower head. The burning glow gripped his vision. After a while his body began to tingle, and his mind drifted like a raven over the grassy hills of time.

***

At first light, a coyote howled, and Cove's brain stirred. He wasn't asleep or awake. He was in that gray zone where his brain was at rest but was beginning to rustle. He was beginning to think. If someone had studied him, they would have watched his slow breathing and concluded he was asleep.

He recalled the remnants of a dream, but it felt different. He wasn't sure if it was really a dream or an apparition that had come from the sage smoke. But like a dream, it was bizarre. He'd been sitting with Leo Terzi, drinking whiskey and talking. The man's eyes were strange. Cove couldn't tell if they were focused on his face or somewhere behind him. The irises were white, and the pupils looked like black peas. The two sat at a table in Terzi's trailer. He couldn't remember what had been said. They each held a highball glass. A bottle of Jack Daniels sat between them. He remembered it had tasted bitter. Terzi's revolver was next to his hand and his pupils were nearly white. The bottle's shadow darkened the pistol. Cove's mind could see the two of them talking, but he couldn't hear the conversation. It was like watching a black and white television with the volume turned down.

He scanned the walls for a clock but none came into view. Neither he nor Terzi looked as if they were enjoying themselves. The discussion looked contentious but not to the point of boiling over. It was good because it wasn't the vivid full-color dreams that were piled with violence and death that had been haunting him, but it was still dominated by Leo Terzi. He questioned whether this was truly a dream, or something he didn't have a name for, because in his memory of this–whatever it was–there were shadows. His other dreams had no shadows.

At some point in the night, he'd crawled into his sleeping bag and Annie had snuggled next to him. He recalled the white smear of the Milky Way in the dark sky and the hooting from down in Gooseberry. Cove reached out and stroked his dog's head. He thought he could feel the burn of whiskey in his mouth and wondered if it was from the dreamlike memory. The air was cool and unmoving on his bare arm. The coyote barked again. He opened his eyes and looked to the west.

Just above the horizon there was a single star in what remained of the night. He dropped his focus to the skyline and followed the earth's edge with his gaze, studying each peak and drainage while mentally breathing their names. Taylor Mountain. Hat Creek. The Salmon River Canyon. The Lemhis. The Pahsimeroi valley. The Big Lost with the edge of Mount Borah sticking up. The Upper Salmon. Van Horn Peak. The West Fork and Morgan Creek Summit. Each piece of ground connected to the other. It was a hundred-mile circle.

He thought about the night and looked over at the half-burned sage stick and the raven wing. His mouth was dry and tasted of the sweet smoke. If it had tasted of whiskey, it was gone now. He reached over to the pack and dug out the water bottle and jerky. Annie's head came up. He took a quick pull on the bottle and then filled his palm and let the dog drink. He took two pieces of jerky out of the bag and gave one to Annie. She wolfed hers down and watched him chew his.

He put on his t-shirt and crawled out of the sleeping bag. He sat down on the rock, and brushed the dirt off his feet with his socks and put his boots on. He stuffed his gear in the pack, stood up and found the stone knife. He felt its edge with his thumb and wondered about the man who had left it here. *Who was he? What demon had he chased on this peak?*

Cove didn't want to leave the relic exposed where someone could find it and pack it off just to stash it in a drawer. The knife belonged here. He stuck it under the corner of the rock he'd used as a stool and covered it with a piece of sagebrush. His fingers felt the butt of his own knife clipped inside his pants pocket. He pulled it out and flicked open the three-inch stainless blade and felt the edge. It was sharper than the stone knife, but about a quarter of an inch of the tip was broken off. Mendiola had found it where Terzi had gone into the river. Cove assumed the tip was still in Terzi's femur. Part of himself urged him to stick it back in his pocket. It'd been his personal symbol of triumph, like Coyote slaying Monster in the time before People. He hesitated, tossed the knife to the ground and headed down the butte.

Chapter 10

As he eased down Gooseberry, the head of Fourth Spring Creek came into view from the other side of Morgan Creek. Cove caught a flash of dust at the top, near the edge of the timber. Stopping, he turned the engine off, brought his binoculars up and studied the spot. An owl hooted from the creek bottom. It was odd that the bird was calling in the daylight. It took Cove back to the night of the half-moon and the boot. There'd been an owl that had boomed its voice at the bark of a fox. There was something about that moment–there seemed to be something about this moment too. Something he couldn't get the coils of his brain around.

Listening for the owl, he studied the head of the creek and watched the spot that had caught his eye. After a minute, he put the binoculars down. Whatever he'd seen had disappeared, and he decided it had probably been the first dust devil of the day.

He found his phone, turned it on and continued down the road. His truck made it another thirty yards before the phone began chiming. He stopped and looked at it. Six missed calls. He opened up the call log. One was from Julie, and the other five were from Mendiola. Fred had left one message. He hit the play button and brought it up to his good ear. "Where you at? We got a hit on the latents. There's a meeting at the SO at three. You need to be here."

He looked up at the top of the ridge and spoke to himself, "No. Fred, I need to find out what's killing the West Fork. Figure out why things are dying. Warden stuff."

His mind flipped a coin. It landed heads-up. He called Mendiola.

"A meeting about what?" Cove asked.

"Where the hell you been?"

"Morgan Creek."

"Who you seeing?" Mendiola asked.

"Ever hunt the West Fork?" Cove asked.

"You need to be here for this."

"Quit dodging the question, Fred. Have you ever hunted it? Ever spent any time in there?"

"Couple of times. Be here at three."

"You know of any old mines up here?" Cove paused for a moment and gave up. "What's this meeting?"

"Juan Torres Rodriguez," Mendiola said it emphasizing each of the three names as if they were a list. "That's Jose. His prints are in the system. He's a Mexican national who isn't supposed to be in the U.S. Did hard time in the federal system for conspiracy to distribute meth. McGee will be here, of course, and DEA's coming from Boise."

"You can have my doughnut. I've got stuff to do."

"McGee said he's gonna try and get the DEA to file a federal subpoena for your informant. Put her in front of the grand jury in Poky."

Cove's head dropped. "I don't think they can do that. How they gonna serve it?"

"I'd guess on you."

"Good luck with that. McGee's blowing smoke. You don't subpoena informants. You subpoena witnesses."

"That's his argument. She's a witness."

Cove thought about the two kids in Armando's yard, and growled to himself. "I'll be there."

He hung up and looked back to the top of Fourth Spring Creek. It was the first feeder creek on the south side of the West Fork, a doglegged timbered gash. There were flat benches with small patches of lighter green aspen. He judged that a pencil line on a map would measure out to be about two miles from the top to the bottom and it'd loose a thousand feet. He also knew the pencil and the map would lie. On the ground, it would be a lot farther than two miles and much tougher. It'd be a round-trip hike that'd take a day. Two miles and a thousand feet up and then back down. In central Idaho, miles meant little when on foot. And that was one of six tributaries he could see in the West Fork. All of a sudden, he didn't have time to check out any of the timbered side drainages that formed the West Fork. Not with this meeting.

He toyed with heading up to top of Morgan Creek and looking for the illegal bear bait. Thinking about the distance, he figured it'd take two hours at the most to find the bait and do whatever needed to be done. He still had the hunch that whoever had done it was using road kills and not deer that had been shot—if that were true, Mike

105

Pallid wasn't going to be interested in prosecuting it—which pissed Cove off even more. *Screw Pallid,* he thought. He turned around and headed for the summit.

***

It was fifteen miles to the top of Morgan Creek. The farther the road climbed, the rougher it got. The vegetation in the drainage changed with the elevation and turned from sagebrush to timber.

It took Cove forty minutes to drive to the summit. At the top, the main road continued and then dropped into Panther Creek. Almost at the divide, Cove found the smaller road his informant had described and turned off into the black timber.

His source had guessed the bait was about a half mile up the road and was located a hundred yards or so off the two-track to the right. The road followed the Lemhi and Custer County boundary. The left side was Lemhi County, and the right side was Custer County. After a quarter mile, Cove could see where someone had been unloading four-wheeled all-terrain vehicles and driving off through the timber. He continued up the road for a couple of hundred yards and parked to avoid leaving vehicle tracks that could raise a red flag for whoever had been placing the bait.

Cove dropped the tailgate and let Annie out of the bed. They angled back into the timber. It was a simple job to locate the bait by following the tracks and listening to the guttural calls from a pair of ravens.

Bear season had started in the middle of April, and would end in a few days. Cove suspected that whoever had hunted over this bait site had placed the deer as soon as the snow was gone and hunted over it throughout the season.

As he got closer, the air was different. It had a touch of rancid meat smell to it. Cove glanced at Annie. Her hackles were up, and it wasn't over the rancid odor. A pile of dead wood had been placed on the bait, and bears had dug through the limbs and poles to get to the food. The poles were marked with the white spots of bird droppings. The bait had been covered with the wood to keep ravens and magpies from getting to it. Cove was a bit on edge because there was a chance they could blunder into a sow with cubs. The worst case scenario would be a bluff charge, probably directed at Annie, from an enraged momma that was willing to put herself at risk for her cubs.

The bait consisted of various parts of mule deer that had been scattered about. The only thing left were the bones and pieces of partially dried deer hide. Everything else had been consumed. He was able to locate nine deer legs and portions of three spinal columns with ribs and attached pelvises. In the center of the mess, there was a large pile of black feces that had deer hair in it.

His mission was to figure out how the deer had died, since that was the root of the legal issue. It wasn't lawful to use deer for bait, but his prosecutor wasn't going to be interested if it turned out they were road kills.

He thought about his theories. The first was that the deer were road kills—they'd been hit on the highway—and the second was that they had been shot closed-season and hauled to this location. Both of these theories involved transporting the carcasses in a pickup truck and then moving them through the timber with the ATVs. It was probably the work of at least two people, since moving three deer would not have been practical for one person.

He examined the spinal columns. Each had the pelvis attached. One still had the skull connected to it. Most of the ribs were still connected to the vertebrae. The U-shape of the pubic arch on the pelvises told Cove that all three were females.

If the animals had been shot, he should be able to find trauma consistent with a projectile through the ribs or vertebrae. Finding none, he located the two disconnected skulls. If they had been shot at night using a spotlight, it would be the norm for the animals to have been hit in the head. He found no bullet trauma in the skulls.

There were several broken bones that appeared to be postmortem. He came to this conclusion since there was no discoloration of dried blood in the pores along the fractures. On one of the carcasses, he found a rib that was broken and still connected. At the edges of the fracture, he could see a dark line caused by blood clotting. He found a fracture in a leg with the same associated clotting along the margins. The fractures were consistent with what a pathologist would call blunt-force trauma. Had the breaks been caused by a feeding bear–postmortem or after death–there would be no bleeding. Cove concluded that whoever had dumped these deer had gathered them along the highway. The irony was that this site was on the wrong side of the hill. They were a few hundred yards into Custer County. Had the deer been dumped to attract bears on the other side of the hill, he would have been standing in Lemhi County, and the case would have been grabbed by a young female prosecutor who possessed a sense of outrage when it came to wildlife violations. Cove's only realistic approach on this bait was to file it away and attempt to find time for it during next year's bear season.

Cove checked his watch. It was almost noon. He could still smell the sage smoke on his skin. It smelled like it belonged. It didn't smell like campfire smoke, but there was no way he was going to sit in a meeting with the DEA, the state police, and the sheriff wondering what he'd been smoking. It was time to head home and get cleaned up.

Chapter 11

As Cove pulled into the parking lot, he spotted Wayne McGee's Jeep Patriot and felt his blood slowing down. While showering, he'd thought about this meeting. He assumed its purpose was to figure out what investigative direction to take on the Mexican national who had been driving a truck that carried the severed foot of an unknown dead man and was associated with a second murder in Arizona. What was clear to Cove was the only dog he had in this fight was to keep his promise to Armando. His planned strategy was to keep his mouth shut and his eyes open like an owl perched in a cottonwood. He didn't have a great deal of confidence with his plan, but he was going to run with it.

He walked into the sheriff's office. Through the back door, he could see Mendiola, McGee and Mike Pallid sitting around the table. Cove took one of two empty chairs across from McGee and caught the smell of cigarettes coming off of Pallid, who was to his right, reviewing a file. The prosecutor didn't bother to acknowledge Cove's arrival. Cove couldn't tell if he was so absorbed with what he was reading or whether it was an excuse to ignore him.

"Mike," Cove said. "How you doing?"

Pallid didn't look up. "Great." It was said with sarcasm.

The prosecutor was wearing black wire rimmed glasses and his combed-over hair was failing at its job of hiding his bald head.

"Thanks for coming, Charlie," Mendiola said.

McGee's phone chimed. He looked down at it. "DEA's just pulling onto Main."

"Where's Jenks?" Cove asked, looking at Fred. "Isn't he part of this thing?"

"Working traffic," Mendiola explained. "This is a bit above his pay grade. Since this thing has escalated, I think ISP and DEA are going to take the lead."

"Escalated?" Cove asked.

"The homicide in Arizona."

Pallid looked up. "Charlie, how'd your informant come up with this information?" His forefinger tapped a report he'd been reading.

"Let's wait until Duran gets here," Mendiola said.

The question made Cove's heartbeat pick up, and he realized keeping restrained like an unblinking owl could become a challenge.

The front door of the office creaked. A female walked through Mendiola's office and pulled up a chair. She looked at Mike Pallid and glanced at Cove. "I'm Special Agent Renee Duran with Drug Enforcement."

She was a tall and slender woman with short blonde hair. She could have been mistaken for a P.E. teacher. She was wearing jeans and an untucked red and white plaid shirt. The sleeves were rolled up, and the front of it was unbuttoned, exposing a white ribbed t-shirt. Cove assumed the shirttail was hiding her duty weapon. He glanced at McGee and caught him staring at Duran's breasts like a bird dog pointing a pheasant.

Mendiola made the introductions.

Duran gave Cove an odd look. "We meet again, the famous Charles Cove."

Cove frowned, not knowing if she'd given him a compliment or was being derisive. He shook his head. "I don't think we've met."

Mendiola broke the sudden quiet. "I'm not sure if you're aware of this, Charlie, but Renee was able to make a couple of arrests after the Terzi case. Figured out who he was getting his meth from and doing some dealing." He nodded. "She interviewed you in the hospital."

"You were squeezing a morphine pump." She smiled. "It wasn't much of a conversation, but it was interesting. You look different."

"The reason I called everybody in," Mendiola explained, "is that we all know a little bit about this case, and there are a lotta different directions it can take. I think there's a possibility there's been a homicide in this county, and that's my prime interest."

"I don't see where you're coming from on that," Pallid said and tapped his pen on the table. "This smells like an Arizona case to me. Rodriguez is obviously connected to a homicide down there. That's probably where the foot came from."

"He'd been here a week," Mendiola said, and looked at Cove. "Charlie, how long do you think it'd been in the cooler?"

Cove rubbed his ear and flicked his eyebrows up. "Good question." He put his elbows on the table, clasped his hands and rubbed his thumbs together in front of his face. "The foot was eleven degrees colder than the air temperature. The ice looked pretty fresh to me, and it'd been laying out there for an hour." He looked at Mendiola. "I assume you've got pictures of it... I'm guessing it'd been in the cooler for a few hours at the most. The boot would have melted the ice and been wet otherwise."

"That's speculation," Pallid said. "We can't use that shit in court."

Mendiola frowned. "This isn't court, Mike. We gotta figure out what happened first. If you read the pathologist's report, it says the same thing more or less."

McGee spoke. "Two to three days. That's what the pathologist said."

"Two days in the cooler?" Pallid asked.

"No," McGee corrected. "He thought that whoever the deceased is–the guy the foot came from–had only been dead for three days at the most." McGee explained. "He's basing it on the lack of bacterial growth and the fact the tissue hadn't been frozen."

"From what I saw," Cove said, "it'd been exposed for two days before it went in the cooler."

"Based on?" Pallid asked.

"The size of the few maggots that had hatched and the smell. It was fresh. It hadn't had a chance to start to decompose," Cove explained. "It'd been in the mid-seventies that week. It wouldn't have taken long to start smelling with those temps. At some time, it had been outside the cooler, and the flies got to it but only long enough for some of the eggs to hatch. That's two days right there, at least in those kind of conditions."

"How long did that thing lay out there at the wreck?" Pallid asked.

"A couple of hours. Maybe more," Mendiola said. "I'd have to look at the log."

"There you go. Maggot mystery solved," Pallid said.

Cove looked at the prosecutor and started to speak, but he held it back. He realized that prosecutor was arguing that there wasn't a Custer County case, and that there was nothing Cove could say to change his stance. He'd heard the same speech before. Pallid wanted this thing to get up and walk away.

Pallid stood up. "You guys find a body, let me know. I've got a hearing at four." He put his pen in his shirt pocket, gathered up a legal pad and walked out the door.

"I'll bet Jose's a long way from here anyway," Cove said.

"Is that what your informant says?" McGee asked.

"No, my source has no idea where he's at." Cove shook his head. "Why would he hang around here? He was in a wreck with a body part and cocaine. He's gotta know the heat's on. I'd guess he's sitting on a beach in Baja."

"Who's this Jose?" Duran asked.

"The name I was using for Rodriguez before we got the AFIS hit." Mendiola nodded and looked at Cove. "Yeah, it'd make sense if he was sitting on a beach somewhere, but it doesn't answer what he was doing here."

McGee looked at Cove. "Who's the guy that busted him out of the hospital?"

Cove swallowed and squeezed the tip of his nose. "My source doesn't know."

Mendiola was now staring at Cove also.

Duran cleared her throat. "When we arrested him in Phoenix seven years ago, Rodriguez was working for the Sinaloa Cartel. That's a club you don't quit. You might have seen it in the news, but we arrested sixty of them last winter. It took three years. It's still in court. Called it Operation Narco Polo. They were running eighty percent of the cocaine, heroin and meth in Chicago. Tons. We ran lots of wiretaps, mostly in California. People think they don't cross the border, and that's bullshit. Idaho came up in some of those phone calls. As part of that, we've identified cartel members in Oregon and Idaho." She paused and looked at McGee. "That stays in this room. Right now they've got a turf war going with the Tijuana Cartel along the border. Our agency obtained a map of California during a warrant that shows whose turf belongs to who. The whole state's carved up."

"We believe there are similar lines drawn in the northwest, but for all I know, Sinaloa claims all of Idaho. Hell, maybe the whole region. Their resources are literally unlimited. They have billions. Historically, if a cartel caught another operating in their territory, they'd kidnap a couple of their narcos and cut their heads off to send a message. With the homicide out of Phoenix, it's clear that they made him as one of our informants, thus the removal of the lips. I'm convinced this severed foot is something similar. Somebody was operating on Sinaloa's territory without their permission." Duran shook her head. "Maybe it was the Tijuanas, maybe the Zetas. I don't know. Maybe freelancers. What you need to understand with the cartels, is that when they control turf, it's like an umbrella. They don't control everyone, but everybody pays to play. If somebody wants to run a meth cook in Baja, that's fine, but they're gonna pay the cartel, and probably pay to move it through them too. The foot's a message." She looked at Cove. "That's why it was in the cooler. He was taking it somewhere. Keep your boots off our ground or pay the piper." Duran looked at Mendiola. "We sit up here in Idaho, and think we're a long way from the border. It's a three-day drive. We're two nights from the border."

Mendiola's eyes narrowed. "So where was he taking the foot?"

Duran shook her head. "We'll probably never know, but in all likelihood, it would have shown up on somebody's doorstep. They do that with severed heads."

"Jesus," Cove said and rubbed his leg.

Duran looked at him and applied a red tube of moisturizer to her mouth. "These guys are real sons of bitches. At the Talavara scene, the lips were gone. I guess you know that. They cut them off and took them. They weren't taken as a fetish like we see with some sexually driven homicides. I'm betting they hung 'em on somebody's door. Our Phoenix office says nobody's talking right now. The severed lips are supposed to be confidential, known only to LEOs working the case, but the snitches all know about them."

McGee looked at Cove. "When Fred called me with the Westbank tip, he said your informant had first-hand knowledge. Tell us about that. How'd she know Rodriguez was in the motel?"

"None of that matters," Cove said, flat-faced. "What matters was that it was good information. She got us his name."

"We need to interview her," McGee said. "Find out what else she knows. Maybe she can finger where Rodriguez is hanging."

"I interviewed her." Cove's voice dropped in pitch. "She knows nothing else." As Cove said it, he thought of the phone call from Mexico he'd left out. For a moment he considered sharing it but kept quiet. He didn't want anything out—in this room or on the street—that could identify Armando.

McGee looked at Duran. "We need to subpoena her. Get her in front of your grand jury in Pocatello." He scowled at Cove. "She may know who the foot belongs to or where the body is. She's a witness. We can cut her a deal. Offer her immunity."

Cove looked at Duran and watched her jaw muscle tighten. He met her eyes and she stared back.

"I'll talk to the U.S. Attorney's Office and see what we can do. The grand jury is a powerful investigative tool."

Cove's head swiveled to McGee. "Sources are my bread and butter. You need to take another look at the photo of the dead guy laying in the desert. The one missing his lips." Cove leaned closer. "My informant is untouchable. The season's closed." His eyes narrowed. "Comprende?"

McGee held Cove's stare and then gave a snort and looked away. Cove stood up and walked out the door. Before he was halfway home, his phone buzzed. He pulled it out. The screen showed "Unknown Caller."

Looking for a diversion, he answered it.

"Cove, it's Duran."

He paused and then responded with a touch of hostility. "Yeah?"

"McGee's full of shit," she said. "I'd like to talk to you away from him. You let me buy you a drink tonight, and I'll deal with him over your informant."

Her frankness was relieving. *The enemy of my enemy is my friend.* "What time?"

***

Jeff Jenks was nestled into a shady spot off the highway below Shotgun Creek. It was his favorite hidey-hole for caching speeders. For all practical purposes, he was as unseen as a goose hunter in a pit-blind. The highway came down a hill and curved to his left. It was easy to back into the cottonwoods and disappear. He'd keep the engine running, the air conditioner on and fall asleep. If the dispatcher called, he'd answer it. If anyone came down the hill at sixty-one or greater, his radar would squeal and tell him somebody was doing six-over the speed limit. He'd have plenty of time to wake, rally and light them up. He loved this part of the job. It was a no-brainer. At times like this, even a caveman could be a deputy.

Jenks was three-quarters into a dream about his wife. When they were dating, she'd take him out on her dad's ranch where she'd made a little castle out of hay bales in a haystack, and they'd kiss there for hours and sometimes she let him touch her breasts. But this dream was way beyond the dating days. They were in the haystack, his pants were down and she was having lunch. It was a wonderful place to be until his radar unit jolted him back to reality.

The rig was a dark blue Dodge Durango. The radar showed that he'd been doing sixty-five. He pulled out behind the SUV and brought the mike to his lips. "Custer, three-two-six. Traffic at about milepost two-seventy." He turned his overheads on and pulled in behind the vehicle. It'd slowed to fifty-five, but wasn't stopping.

Juan Torres Rodriguez saw the deputy before he had pulled out of the brush. He slowed down and watched the vehicle approach through his rearview mirror. When the flashing blue lights came on, he pulled the Beretta out of the console, flipped the safety off and slid the 9MM under his right thigh. His concern was that he'd never seen the officer who had caused his wreck, and it was possible that this officer would recognize him. He reached over and grabbed the straw cowboy hat that Barreras had left on the seat, put it on and snugged it down. He fished out the envelope from the console and looked at the Oregon driver's license. In a few moments he was going be Carlos Carpia Cerdos. He lipped a Marlboro, lit it with his Bic and took a long drag. It was time to deal with this matador and own the ring.

Jenks hit his yelp siren, and the vehicle in front of him continued at fifty-five. He was on the verge of declaring a pursuit when the brake lights came on. He turned the siren off, pulled the mike from his lap and pushed the transmit button. "Custer, three-two-six. I'll be out with this vehicle at about two-sixty-five. Plates obstructed with mud. One aboard."

Rodriguez parked just outside the white line. Jenks parked straddling the line to protect him from other vehicles. Just like he'd done a thousand times.

As he approached the SUV, he glanced at the plate. It looked like it had been slapped with a cup full of mud. He stopped just short of the driver's door. The window was down, and the driver's elbow came out in a relaxed fashion.

"Could you turn the engine off for me?" Jenks said it like there was no room for discussion.

Rodriguez caught the baby-faced officer's blue eyes. "Ola, señor. No hablo English. No mucho."

Jenks pointed at the hood of the Dodge and motioned as if he were slashing his throat. He didn't attempt to tell the man to put out the cigarette. There was enough of a language barrier without complicating things.

At the deputy's gesture, Rodriguez couldn't help but crack a smile. "Si señor. Entiendo." He paused and said, "Hertz, Hertz." He turned the engine off and handed Jenks the driver's license and rental document.

Rodriguez watched the deputy's eyes drop down to the documents. The officer was as relaxed as if he were reading the Sunday Times on his couch. Rodriguez's hand reached to his thigh, gripped the pistol under it and at that moment he knew he owned this man's soul. A hint of trouble, and he'd take the guy. Shoot right into one of his gringo-blue eyes. He whispered, "Santa Muerte, gracious a ti."

Jenks glanced up. The Mexican looked friendly enough; he was smiling. The deputy had no idea he was looking at the face of death. "Yeah, Hertz. I get it. One momento, Mr. Credos." He turned, walked back to his patrol vehicle and got in.

Jenks called in the information on the driver's license. He examined the rental papers. Carlos Carpia Credos had rented the vehicle in Portland ten days ago. The rental papers were proof of insurance. He didn't see a problem.

Rodriguez studied the deputy from the Durango's side mirror, while smoking his cigarette. The cop had turned his back on him and walked as if he were a bartender who was going to return with an ice cold tequila. There hadn't been any vehicles pass on the highway. If this went another two, maybe three minutes, he was going to slip the gun into his pants next to his spine, walk back to the deputy's rig and with his no-comprende bullshit-routine, put a bullet in one of the gringo's blue eyes.

Jenks sat behind the steering wheel and looked at the photo on the license. A round-faced Hispanic man stared back with a mustache. But the guy that had given him the license was smooth shaved and had two black eyes. Jenks scratched inside his ear and took a toothpick from his cup holder and stuck it in his mouth. The man in the photo looked younger. Moving the toothpick to the other side of his lips, he thought about it and frowned. Somebody had cold-cocked him. He shook his head. *Mexicans.*

The dispatcher came on. "Three-two-six, your DL's valid, no wants."

Rodriguez gripped the 9MM under his leg and watched the deputy approach. He was holding the driver's license and rental paper in his left hand, and his right hand was free to grab his gun. *Was this a trick? Santa Muerte, should I kill him now?*

When Jenks got to the window, Rodriguez leaned out, hiding his right hand that still gripped the Beretta. Saliva came to his mouth, and it tasted like death. Jenks offered the license and document. Rodriguez took them with his left hand and looked at the toothpick in the cop's mouth. It was a sign of disrespect. *Maybe I'll shoot him in the mouth first.*

"Mr. Credos. You need to slow down."

Rodriguez lips turned down, and his head turned.

Jenks's put his palm out and moved it up and down like he was patting a dog. "Slow. El comprendo?"

Rodriguez's lips resumed the wide smile that showed his nicotine stained teeth, but his eyes were full of blood. His right hand tightened on the gun under his leg. For perhaps fifteen seconds, he didn't respond. Finally he said, "Si, mi amigo. Slow."

Chapter 12

When Cove walked into his house, his phone growled like a bear. The deep raspy ringtone alerted him to the fact that it was his boss, George Nayman. After hesitating, he slid his finger across the screen and brought to his ear.

"Charlie, you figure out what killed those fish?"

"Not yet, waiting on the lab. Bob had me send in a water sample."

"I'm betting it's some disease." Nayman said. "Something like that parasite that was killing whitefish last fall."

"I found two dead mergansers too."

"Well," George said, "maybe they aren't supposed to eat dead fish."

"I can't believe eating fish'd kill a merganser."

"I found one once with a big ol' spinner in his mouth. The asshole that hooked it probably thought it was funniest goddamned thing he'd ever seen. Looked like it'd starved to death."

"I don't think Bob believes it's disease. He's thinking it's a mine leaching into the creek. I'm going to try to find it."

"How many fish you find?"

Cove paused, "I think seven."

"Two ducks and a limit of trout," George said. "Dax's got problems upriver. Keeps finding salmon guts in the Holman hole."

"All's he's gotta do is get his butt outta bed and go work it. That kid'll work late, but morning's a creek he's never been up."

"You need to go show him how to work it."

"He needs to learn how to make coffee first."

"Anyway," George said, "enough time spent on a few dead fish. Give Dax a hand. Go park your ass in the willows with him. Maybe show him how to flake arrowheads."

After the call, Cove bit his lip and thought about the West Fork and the issue his boss had just talked about. The Holman hole was a large pool in the Salmon River that held Chinook salmon like firewood in a woodcutter's lot in late June and July. In the early morning, you'd sit on the cliff and watch the big fish tailing near the surface. Some of them pushed twenty-five pounds. The hole was upriver from Challis at the mouth of Holman Creek, about ten miles below Sunbeam. Dax Sparks was the new officer in Stanley, and it was in his patrol area.

Cove believed that working the hole entailed one secret—getting your ass out of bed before the crooks did.

He took a tall glass out of his cabinet, filled it with ice and retrieved a bottle of Jack Daniel's from the top of his refrigerator. He poured the amber liquid over the cubes and took a swallow.

Picking up his phone, he selected Dax's phone number and waited for him to answer.

"Evening. George says you've got problems in the Holman hole."

"Yeah, somebody keeps cleaning salmon, but I can't find anybody using heavy gear."

"They do it at first light." Cove hesitated. "I thought I'd mentioned it when you were moving to Stanley."

"Probably did. I've got bear problems up the ying-yang."

"It's yin-yang. There's always bear problems up there. Here's what's worked for me. You have to get up there in the dark. About four-thirty, stash your truck up Holman Creek. There's usually somebody camped in there, but you won't wake 'em. Walk down the creek and cross the highway. Take your headlamp. You've got to get set up before they get there, and they'll show at first light. There's an old ditch down in the willows you can watch from. Take a pot of coffee. My beater lawn chair should still be there."

"Other than getting out of bed, sounds easy enough."

Cove took another drink. "It can be. The problem is, if they shag a salmon and run for their rig, they'll be outta there before you can get to 'em, and your rig's up the creek. Don't ask how I know."

"I'll keep you posted."

"Hey, and do me a favor. George is expecting me to work it with you. He's going to ask. I've got something cooking down here. Tell him you wanted to work it by yourself."

***

Cove fed Annie and changed from his uniform into a

pair of faded blue Levi's. He slipped his five-shot Smith and Wesson snubbed-nose revolver into an inside-the-pants holster and secured it behind the point of his right hip. He felt naked without a knife and fished out a new three-inch Kershaw folder, still in the box, from his gun safe and clipped it inside his pants pocket. He slipped a dark khaki t-shirt over his torso and left it untucked, concealing the gun. The bars in Challis had a reputation for a fight-a-week during the summer, but it'd been three or four years since there'd been any gunfire. Cove had made a lot of friends as a game warden, but he was a realist. He'd also made his enemies, and finding one in a bar, stoked on alcohol, was a bad mix. Bars were not a place he could relax.

He parked his old Tundra pickup under a street light down from the Borah Bar. There was a couple sitting on the porch sharing a bottle of Budweiser and a cigarette. The guy was skinny and had a full beard with long gray hair that curled below his ball cap. The female was a barefoot heavy-set woman with jeans that had been cut off just below her crotch. Her red tank top was a size too small and stretched over her large breasts. She had long stringy blonde hair with a half-inch of brown roots showing. As Cove approached, the female smiled at him, and exposed a mouthful of crooked teeth.

Cove recognized the man. He'd pinched him two or three winters ago for a trapping violation. The man had illegally snared a mountain lion in a coyote set, and he'd tried to launder it as a lawfully killed animal so he could sell the hide.

"Jack, you still in Mackay?" Cove asked

The guy studied him for a moment. "That you, Cove? You undercover? How the fuck ya doing?" He said it with a friendly slur. "Sorry about that cat," the man said. "Lemme buy ya a beer." He started to get up but stumbled back down.

"Water over the dam," Cove said. "Next time call me. Save us both a heap of trouble." Cove stepped around him. "You see a deputy coming up the street, hide the beer."

Cove walked into the darkened room. From the jukebox, a female voice was singing an upbeat love song that Cove didn't recognize. He heard her chorus something about *shaking it off*. Other than that, the place was quiet. It smelled of stale cigarettes and beer. A slender cowboy sat at the polished wooden bar and didn't look up. He was wearing a long sleeved plaid shirt. His dark hair was mashed down from a day of wearing a wide-brimmed hat that rested beside him on the bar. In front of him was a pack of Camel's and a bottle of Budweiser. There was a mirror on the wall behind the bar that was rimmed by bottles of liquor. Cove could see the man watching him in the reflection.

The room had a dozen tables in it. Each one had a candle on it, and most were lit. Cove picked a table in a corner at the end of the room and sat down facing the bar. The bartender appeared from a side doorway. She was in her early forties with sandy hair that met her shoulders. Cove couldn't remember her name, but remembered she'd been in the bar the last time he was there. She was hard to forget. She'd been wearing a low cut tank top that showed off a spider-web tattoo that lived between her saline enhanced breasts. It'd been quite the show. Tonight the tatt was covered with a pink top that didn't hide her nipples. She saw Cove, grabbed a towel and walked over to him and smiled.

"Charlie, it's been a while. You alone tonight?"

He swallowed. "Meeting somebody." *Sometimes this town is too small.* At the thought, Renee Duran walked through the door, came over and sat down. She had lost the plaid shirt and was wearing a sleeveless white v-neck that exposed her summer tan. A pair of red rimmed glasses highlighted her slender face.

She turned to the bartender. "You know how to do a Texas Two Step?"

The bartender shook her head and frowned. "I'm not supposed to dance with customers."

Duran chuckled. "Make it a margarita then." She caught Cove studying her.

"I'll have a Jack on the rocks with a lime," Cove said.

Duran gave him the same odd look she'd given him at the start of the meeting.

"Thanks for coming, Charlie." She glanced at the bartender and fingered her short blonde hair. "I'll bet she thinks I'm gay. The Texas Two Step's a drink..." She looked back at Cove. "I hate sitting in a motel room. I'm on the road too much. Cable TV drives me nuts. I was glad McGee had to get back to Idaho Falls. He wasn't wearing his ring today." She smiled. "So thanks."

"McGee's nuts if he thinks I'm going to give up a name."

She met Cove's eyes. "I need to talk to an informant."

He stiffened. "No——"

She flashed her white teeth and shook her head.

"Somebody I developed when I was working on the Terzi case."

The conversation lulled as the bartender approached and set their drinks down. "I just looked up what a Texas Two Step was. I thought you were hitting on me."

"Sometimes it's a dance. Sometimes it's a pickup line," Duran said, smiling. "Tequila's fine."

When the bartender left, Duran continued. "I liaison with Homeland Security. They've got an intel center in Boise. I coordinate their drug stuff." Duran stirred her drink with a plastic swizzle stick and took a sip. "My source is clean. Hasn't used since you took Terzi down. I hope that's true anyway. I just want to touch bases and cultivate her. She might know what Rodriguez was doing here. She still knows the players. If a Mexican's been bringing a load of shit through once in a while, she may have heard something. I'll talk to her and then head up to Salmon and then the Bitterroot. Talk to the locals–see if they've heard anything."

"I should have been looking for dead fish today, not sitting in a meeting with McGee."

She took a sip. "If Rodriguez had muled a load to Missoula and was headed south, there shoulda been bunch of cash found at the wreck. It flows both ways." She looked at Cove. "You didn't see a duffle bag or anything did you?"

Cove thought about the wreck and realized what she was implying. "If Jenks found cash, it'd be in evidence, and you'd know about it."

"I'm not accusing anybody," Duran nodded. "I don't think he brought a load up. I think he's a fixer.

Cove's head rotated. "Fixer?"

"That's what he was doing with the foot. He fixes problems. The desecration of Talavera's face and this amputated foot aren't a coincidence. They tell him something's broken, and he takes care of it. His boss told him Talavara was flapping his lips. He killed him, cut his lips off and used his ID and credit card to rent the truck to come up here to fix something else. Somewhere in between, he delivered the lips." She took her glasses off. "I hate these things, but the pollen's bugging my contacts." She took a sip of her drink. "Part of the mystery is whether there's a connection between the Talavara murder and this foot. It's hard to say. I'm guessing since they are so far apart, they're not connected."

Cove watched her take another sip. She looked as fresh as if she'd just gotten out of the shower. Her pale blue eyes were deeper, framed by a touch of makeup that he didn't recall from the meeting. She had the edge of a smile and looked relaxed.

"You said you wanted to talk with me away from McGee."

She nodded and put her glass down. "I'd like to pick your brain about the foot and some other things. The pathologist's report was too clinical. It mentioned there was blood spatter on the boot. He didn't send any photos with his report so I haven't seen what he's talking about. You notice the blood?"

Coves eyebrows flicked up. "It was kind of weird. I remember seeing the blood on the boot before my brain accepted there was a severed foot in it." He took a sip of his whiskey. It was rich with the flavors of oak and charcoal, and the vapor permeated into his nose and windpipe. "I'm always looking for blood on people's boots. I think that's what drew my attention from the stump..." Cove looked around the bar and his voice lowered. "I got a call one night from a landowner. They'd seen a vehicle working a light, and then they'd heard a shot. It was after midnight, and I lit up the first truck coming down the drainage. The guy gave me a bullshit story about not being able to sleep. I looked in the back of his truck, and it was clean, no blood, just a garbage can. He was by himself, and I couldn't see a rifle, but I could smell alcohol. He had to be the shooter. Had him step out so I could run a field sobriety test and buy some time. I thought there might be a second vehicle that was watching the stop from up the drainage. Sometimes they'll run two vehicles like that. I had him do the one-legged stand. There was fresh blood on both boots. He claimed he'd had a nose bleed. I found the spotlight and rifle behind his seat. There was a freshly gutted whitetail fawn and rubber gloves in the garbage can. The bed of the truck was clean. It was quite the poacher's trick. Pull the can out, throw the fawn in, load up and go. Other than the boots, no blood. I figured he'd been doing the trick for years. Who's gonna look in a garbage can for a deer?"

"DUI?"

"Yeah, I hooked him. Jenks ran the Intoxilyzer, and he blew a point one-four. Pallid let him plead to the deer, and he walked on the DUI. It was his second one."

Cove felt like she was leading him down a path and had used the blood drop to get him talking. "You said you wanted to talk about McGee?"

Duran shook her head. "I'm surprised Pallid can win an

election."

"It's easy," Cove said. "Nobody runs against him. The only other attorney here is an old fart who doesn't spend much time in his office."

"Do you think the blood came off the chainsaw?"

He studied her face, wondering where this was going. She looked inviting. The candle between them flickered. She seemed to have turned on her sexuality. *Had she done this to get him to trip and fall? Was there something afoot that was beyond the McGee problem?*

"No," Cove answered. "No way. It was about this wide." He held up his thumb and forefinger about a half-inch apart. "It was teardrop shaped. The tail pointed back towards the guy's leg. I'd guess it came from about knee high. I don't know." He shook his head. "If he'd taken a round through his hand–a defensive wound–I suppose it could have come from that." Cove squinted one eye and sighed. "If the body had been vertical–hung from a tree or whatever–the blood could have dripped off the chainsaw, but then it would've been round, not teardrop shaped and besides, this guy was dead when the chainsaw hit him. There was no blood in the wound. I'm sure it was sawn off after he was dead." Cove rubbed his thigh. "Weird shit." He studied her face and wondered why she had wanted to meet with him. She was attractive, but she'd stepped it up for this meeting. What did she want?

"That's the first thing I looked for in the pathologist's report. It *was* postmortem. I'd assumed they'd whacked the leg off while the guy was still alive... *Fuck.*" She coughed it out. "These bastards do this shit all the time. They film the beheadings. They're all over the Internet.

They're worse than Isis in Syria. There's at least one video of a beheading with a chainsaw. They always make them talk first. You can tell they know what's happening." She rubbed her throat. "These guys are horrific. Need a good nightmare? Google it some time."

Cove's tongue moved back and felt the sharp edge of the molar that Terzi's gun barrel had chipped.

"Tell me about the boot," Duran said. "How old was it?"

"It'd been worn for a long time... How serious is McGee about this subpoena?"

"The guy musta been a worker bee." Duran nodded. "Not high up on the food chain. Maybe an illegal they picked up."

Cove noticed she'd dodged the question again, but he went on. "I was wondering if he wasn't a vet. Somebody who'd worn the boot in the military."

"I thought about that too, but I don't think so. Odd thing, there wasn't a sock on this foot." She took a sip and looked at Cove.

How'd I miss that? Cove asked himself.

"I can't imagine working in the sands of the Middle East and not wearing socks." She said. "I hit my boss up on that. He said that sometimes they'd pull their socks in Viet Nam if they were slogging in the rice paddies. Said they were always getting jungle rot. He didn't believe the guys fighting in the sand would go without them."

Cove's eyes narrowed. "This thing gets weirder every day. I've been assuming it belongs to a male. I remember seeing hair on the skin. I guess I shouldn't assume anything like that." Cove rubbed his neck. "Could it be female?"

"Could be. I told McGee they should run DNA to make sure. Sometimes you've got to put a chain around his neck and lead him around like a dog. I've worked with some great investigators with ISP, and he's not on the list. I'm wondering if they haven't given him a shovel. Speaking of assumptions, did the skin look Latino?"

Cove swirled his drink, the ice made a clanking sound, and he thought for a moment. "It was pale. I've seen dead Indians but not Mexicans. I wasn't thinking about that. Was thinking about the chainsaw. The skin was chalky. Could've been. I don't know."

A couple came through the door. Cove looked up. They were in their late twenties; both wore nylon shorts and sandals. They were tan and had muscular arms and legs. The sun had lightened their hair. Cove guessed they were river guides. As they sat down at a table, the female leaned over and whispered something to the man and he smiled.

Cove frowned and looked at Duran. "You know... we're not normal. You ever think about that?"

She looked over at the couple. "What do you mean?"

"They've come in here for fun; they're enjoying themselves. You and I are sitting here talking about a severed foot. Normal people don't do this stuff. Hell, normal people don't even know about this shit." He looked at Duran's ring finger. It was bare. He lowered his voice. "Don't take this wrong, but you're not married, are you?"

"I'll take it anyway I want. But no, not anymore." She glanced back at the couple and met Cove's eyes. "Been there, done that." She brought her glass to her lips and set it back down. "I could get addicted to this shit... What ever happened to Julie Lake?"

Cove wondered if this was a loaded question. "Took a job in Boise."

"I heard she moved in with you."

He'd guessed right and nodded his head. "For a while."

Cove tipped his glass up and slid an ice cube into his mouth. For a moment, he chewed on it and thought about the weeks fogged by dreams filled with pain and pills and the first visits from his demon. The feeling of waking up sweating and feeling her arm on his waist. His eyes stared at his drink while his mind wandered through a dark alley.

After a moment, he looked up. "Fred tell you that?"

"Maybe."

Cove hesitated. "When I was in the hospital, Fred took her over to her house. Terzi's tracks were still in the snow. She told Fred she thought they were fresh." He shook his head. "Somebody'd stapled cardboard over the hole in her door, but everything else was the same. She saw her bedroom and vomited."

Duran frowned. "I guess I can understand. When'd she move to Boise?"

"Maybe it'd been different if somebody'd cleaned the place up. Put everything back where it belonged," Cove explained. "Replaced the door."

The woman at the other table laughed, and Cove looked over at the two. The guy was smiling and had his phone out. He was holding it horizontally and kept moving his finger across the screen as if he were showing photos. He'd swipe and then tell her something.

"The whole thing was a recipe for a train wreck." Cove paused, still watching the couple. "I understand why she left."

"Christ, Charlie, I need another drink after that."

He took the lime from his drink, squeezed it and watched the juice drip into what was left of his whiskey. He brought it to his lips and finished it. "I need to get going."

"Stick around. I've got one more thing I want to pass by you." She turned and caught the waitress's eye. "We'll take another round."

Her statement caught Cove's attention. This was going to be the pitch.

The front door creaked and Cove looked up. A man in his forties walked in and looked over at their table. An oval silver rodeo buckle was cinched to his belt. For a moment the guy stopped and locked eyes. Cove thought he looked familiar and gave a slight nod. He was short, but had a big chest and muscled arms and looked like he made a living bucking hay or building fence. He sat down at the bar, took his ball cap off and exposed a skull that was closely barbered. The man's pause had caught Cove's attention.

"You two have a history?" Duran asked.

"I'm not sure."

The bartender set their drinks down and put her hand on Duran's shoulder. "I assumed you wanted another margarita."

"I wanted a dance," Duran said.

After she'd left, Cove asked. "Are you...?"

Duran gave him her odd look. It was if her eyes were smiling, but the rest of her face was frowning. "You never know."

"Hmm..." Cove murmured and reached for his whiskey.

"I'm messing with you," Duran said, "I'm as straight as a corkscrew is twisted."

Cove felt her knee touch his, and he moved his leg away. He ran the phrase through his head, *straight as a corkscrew is twisted* and wondered if the whiskey was clouding his brain.

"I wanted to talk to you about your informant."

Cove squinted his eyes and leaned towards Duran. His jaw was set and he looked into her eyes. He spoke in a deep low voice. "I'm not giving up my source. She hasn't broken any law. McGee can go *fuck himself* and you––."
He felt her hand squeeze his forearm.

She shook her head. "No. That's not what this is about. This's typical McGee bullshit. There's no way the AUSA's office would do it and there's no way I'd be involved in it. He can't even talk to a federal prosecutor without getting an agent onboard. The AUSA's office'd laugh. They don't force officers to give up sources unless there's one hell of a good reason. The guy's a fucking moron sometimes."

Cove looked at her fingers resting on his arm. They were slender, and the nails were clear and shiny and cut with just the hint of a point. Her tanned skin looked oiled and was curiously wrinkled around her knuckles.

"What do you want?"

"I want to throw something out."

Cove exhaled and took his arm away. His hands palmed his drink.

"If your informant knows too much," Duran said, "he's dead."

The word *he* set Cove back. He felt like he'd been hit with a stick across his face. His eyes flashed left and right.

"She's a *she*."

"I did the math." Duran nodded and watched his eyes. "It was the photo. I couldn't come up with any other theory. And then McGee asked you who the guy was pushing the wheelchair... I watched you like a hawk. Your nose was a foot long. Charlie, you're a shitty liar."

Cove exhaled. He pursed his lips and swallowed. His voice dropped to a near-whisper, and he glanced at the bar. "My informant has three little kids and a wife. The cartel knows about 'em. That was the leverage. He doesn't have any other information. I'll burn in hell before I give him up."

"That's what I'm worried about. Your informant may be more valuable to these devils dead than alive." She leaned in and glanced at the other table to make sure they hadn't drawn attention. Their faces were close, and Cove caught a whiff of something that smelled like cinnamon.

She dropped her voice. "If he knows where the body is, they'll kill him and probably his family too. That's the way they roll. If he knows where it's at, and is willing to give up the location to you, we can put him and his family in witness protection. Get 'em the hell out of here. Without the body, this case isn't going to get made."

"He's got no clue about anything else. Leave him alone." He looked over at the couple. Their legs were touching under the table.

"Works for me," she said. "That's the last time I ever bring it up. I'll tell McGee to go swing on a rope." She sat back and sipped her drink.

The bartender was talking to the men at the bar. The three broke into a deep chorus of a laugh.

After a moment Duran spoke. "Fred says you're Salish."

Cove rubbed his earlobe. "Usually says I'm Flathead, but yeah. My mother's white. I think I have her nose and chin... and her values." He took another drink and watched the female bartender talking to the two patrons. "Sometimes I think I'm Anglo. My informant used the word gringo, and I didn't know if he was talking about me or what. I can't speak Salish. My grandfather could." Cove set his drink on the table and rolled his palms out. "So am I Salish? Sometimes I wonder."

"You didn't mention your father."

"Died when I was in high school. He caught hell for marrying my mother." He picked his drink up and took a swallow. "I probably knew my grandfather better than my dad. He knew a lot about the old days. I was stupid and didn't listen much."

Duran nodded. "I started school as a history major. I was hoping to do my master's thesis on Lewis and Clark. I read the journals and the authors that interpreted them— so I know a bit about the Salish."

Cove frowned. "DEA hires history majors?"

"That was the thing. I didn't want to teach. I'd had a crush on William Clark when I was a kid. I got to play Sacagawea in ninth grade. Had to wear a wig. It was black with long braids. I've still got it." She nodded. "I figured out I needed something else. My dad was a cop, so I switched to criminology. It cost me another year and a half in school." Duran picked up her drink and held it towards Cove. "So, here's to the Salish for saving my old boyfriend, William Clark."

Cove brought his drink up and clicked on hers but didn't smile. His wrinkles deepened. "I've read lots about the early American west. It's something I do. This Lewis and Clark stuff is... kind of curious." He set his drink down and stared at the chunks of ice covered in bubbles and yellow liquid for a moment. The flame from the candle shifted.

"My mom's favorite expression is that *every river has two sides*. Two banks. What she means is there are two ways of looking at everything. It's the same with Lewis and Clark." Cove took a sip of his Jack and ran his fingers through his dark hair. "It marked the beginning of the western movement of the European culture. You know that. But people in this country don't look at it from the Indian side of the river and you won't find much written about it."

Cove swirled the ice around and listened to it clinking against the sides of the glass. He brought it to his mouth, swallowed the whiskey and felt the fire settle in his gut. "The Salish had lived on their land for thousands of years. From the Bitterroot to the Yellowstone. Over ten thousand." He looked up at Duran. "The French sold the land—the Louisiana Purchase. They'd never walked on it. Never looked at it. And yet they claimed it was theirs. I'd like to see the deed they'd made up. It's bizarre on its face. But anyway... as you know—that's what kicked off the Lewis and Clark expedition. It was the start of an invasion. When my grandfather's ancestors found them in the Bitterroot, it was the beginning of the end." He looked into her pale blue eyes. "It *was* the end."

"Ouch," Duran said. The corners of her eyes broke into

a frown. "I guess I won't try that line on you again."

Cove's tongue found his chipped tooth. For a moment he toyed with ordering another whiskey, but he stood up. "Next time bring your wig. It might work." He nodded and his dark eyes smiled. "Travel safe."

Chapter 13

Cove snapped awake. He wanted to lunge for the Glock on the nightstand, but he froze, held his breath and listened. The only thing he could hear was his heart booming in his chest. Annie was quiet. Exhaling, he wrote it off as another dreamless terror and massaged his temples. He didn't want to look at the clock, but he glanced over. It was 3:43. For some bizarre reason, he'd awoken and seen those three red glowing numbers many times. 3:43. It'd happened over and over. 3:43. The only person he'd told was Julie. Her eyes had widened and then she'd looked away and didn't want to talk about it. His brain had a locked-in video of her reaction and he believed she knew something and was keeping it to herself.

He threw his sweats on and made a pot of coffee. After he let Annie out, he turned on his computer. When it booted up, he clicked on Google Earth. In the search field, he typed in "Challis, Idaho" and watched as the image zoomed into the tiny town. It seemed to center on Third Street. Right above the red roof of Julie's old house. He looked at the clock at the bottom of the screen and expected it to read 3:43. It was 5:05.

He poured a mug of coffee and sat back down. He

noticed he had an unopened email. He clicked on it. It was short and from Bob Johnson. *"Lab says they should have the tests done tomorrow. Have you found any more fish?"*

He responded. *"No more dead fish. Not sure if that's good or bad. I should be up there today poking around unless the phone rings."*

He closed his email program, reopened Google Earth, scrolled the satellite image north to Morgan Creek. For a moment, he moved the image to the Cat's Ears and zoomed in to the point where he'd spent the night. He could see the faint trail that led to the top. The rock with the pictographs on it. He had the urge to return to the butte and confront his demon. Biting his lip, he zoomed out and followed the green riparian zone to the confluence of the West Fork.

The tributary ran roughly west to east. On Google Earth, the mouse pointer was the white graphic of a hand the size of a pencil eraser. As he slid it across the drainage, numbers below the screen flashed up and down, rattling off the elevation where the hand hovered. The creek's headwaters started at 8,900 feet, and through its ten-mile course, it dropped over 3,000 feet where it dumped into Morgan Creek.

The north side of the drainage was generally bare and covered with grass and sage. It was cut by several steep gullies that cut the sheer slope at even spaces as if it'd been laid out with a ruler. Looking at the vegetation in the draws, he doubted if any of these would have running water. It was something he hadn't been paying attention to when he'd driven up the road looking for the hypothetical dump site. It was something he'd have to check out. The exception was Blowfly Creek, which was on the upper end of the drainage, and he knew it ran water all summer.

The south side of the West Fork drainage was much bigger and was covered with timber. The largest creek on that side was the East Fork. Cove found the creek's name puzzling. It lacked character. He wondered if the same person had named the West Fork. Perhaps the person had just gazed up from its mouth, never exploring it and not planning to stick around long. Certainly not long enough to see a bear or a lion or lightning hit a tree or some other event worth naming a creek over. Something more meaningful than the relationship to a compass needle.

Just above the East Fork, at the confluence of Blowfly Creek, the drainage was roadless. Cove zoomed out and realized that this wilderness section ate up at least half of the entire area of the basin. He used the measuring function of Google Earth's feature and came up with an area about fifteen square miles with no road access. He knew it fairly well. Three Novembers ago, he and his boss had done a horse trip into this steep country. Cove had located a truck and horse trailer parked at the trailhead, and the plate had come back to a man that had a history of killing over-limits of game. The two wardens had thrown together their gear and horses and headed in the following day. When he and George had gotten near the top of the drainage, they'd pitched two backpack tents in a side draw and although it'd been cold, they'd never lit a fire. They'd spent three days in the basin, working out of the camp and following horse tracks. On the last day, they'd climbed above timberline and crossed over the divide into the Camas Creek drainage.

They'd found the two-man party outside a canvas wall tent at White Goat Lake. The two hunters had seemed friendly enough and had invited the wardens into their tent for coffee. They'd tied their horses away from the hunter's pack string and had sat down on offered camp chairs in the tent while the hunters sat on their cots and complained of wolves ravaging the game herds, and the lack of tracking snow.

Cove had felt that something wasn't right; there was an insincerity in their hospitality. Annie had sat at the opening of the tent, listening to the conversation. Cove noticed her nose kept flaring, tasting the air coming up from Camas Creek. She'd been curiously absorbed by an odor that his nose hadn't been able to touch.

When the two wardens had remounted, Cove caught George's eye, and they reined their horses down the hill following Annie. Seventy five yards below the camp, they found a mule deer doe, gutted and laying on the ground, covered with fresh pine boughs. The hunting season was open only to bucks, and the lack of antlers explained why the animal was hidden. The cuts along both sides of the spine—the back straps—had been stripped. The meat in contact with the ground had soured. When they'd confronted the two hunters, they rolled over. Cove recalled the older man looking at his boots and explaining it away, "It's was just camp meat, we was gonna eat it."

Cove's eyes refocused on the computer screen. He had two horses pastured above his house if he needed them. But what he couldn't envision was riding them up a creek that was poison. There was the old saying that you could lead a horse to water, but you couldn't make it drink. He also knew that you couldn't keep a horse from drinking when it was dry.

He considered this problem and thought about Bob Johnson's toxic mine hypothesis. He concluded that if the prospectors had found anything worthwhile, there'd still be roads. And there weren't any. So he doubted this unspoiled part of the drainage was producing the toxins—assuming Johnson's mine hunch was correct.

He decided to start from the bottom of the West Fork and work up. He'd do it virtually on the computer first, and then he'd pound it with his boots. Since the north side of the creek was barren of trees, that's where he'd start. At least with the computer.

He centered the image south of the creek, changed the aspect of the flat image to the program's three-dimensional view and looked north. The terrain jumped alive. It looked like he was down low, staring at the north ridge with its spurs angling into the bottom. Zooming in, he began studying the surface, looking at the topography and the shadows cast by the vegetation. He stared at features on the screen and slowly moved the view of the earth with the mouse.

Cove wondered what his grandfather would think if he could watch him drag the images of earth across the computer screen, zooming in and out of the hills and creeks with a click. He didn't think he'd approve. To the Salish, the earth was everything. It was holy. Everything came from it and everything returned. Part of the great circle. And here he was, dragging the planet around like it was nothing. Or at least its image.

About a mile upstream, he found a mine shaft. It was in

the head of a draw with a steep bald face. Almost at the top and easy to catch. The shadows of the aerial photograph didn't lie. Somebody had hacked a rough road down from the nearby spur ridge. He could see the light gray tailings next to the dark spot he believed was the mouth of the drift. It couldn't be anything else. Bright green vegetation showed that a spring had developed around this disturbed spot, but it appeared that the dump pile itself was oddly devoid of plants.

Cove studied the gully below the mine, but it looked as dry as a rock. It probably wasn't the source that was killing the creek. Nonetheless, it was a lead. Plus it gave him confidence that what he was doing with Google Earth was viable and that it could help narrow down his ground search. The mine and the gully it sat in was a place he needed to check out.

He retrieved a Forest Service map and spread it out on his floor. He found the corresponding spot on the map and marked it with a yellow "X," using a grease pencil. Back at the computer, he zoomed back out and found a two-track road that led from the bottom of the West Fork road, cutting off through the sagebrush to the top of the divide. On top, it paralleled the creek and ended above the mine. He also noted the date the image had been uploaded by Google. It was a year old. The area around Challis was known for its earthquakes. It was possible that since the photo had been taken, the flow of the spring coming out of the mine had increased, and it was now making its way into the West Fork.

He moved up the drainage and studied a similar colored belt of rocks in a steep cliff, but found no evidence of a shaft. In the next draw over, he found what looked like an ATV trail that went to a possible mine, but the vegetation didn't change. Studying the shadows, he couldn't find anything that resembled tailings. A few hundred yards west, he found surface scarring from what had to be mining but again there was no tell-tale change in vegetation.

He zoomed into Blowfly and studied the timber. If a road had been cut in, it might show through the canopy, but he found nothing of interest.

Moving back to the bottom of the West Fork, he crossed the creek and started with the first drainage. It was Fourth Spring Creek. He'd been to the top of the drainage but had never hiked down into it. Examining it from the image on Google Earth, he was again challenged by the timber hiding the surface. What held promise was the road that led along the drainage's flank that had been laid outside the timber in the sagebrush. It was much more substantial than the two-track roads that dotted the sagebrush. The road had switchbacks that had been cut with a cat. At some point, somebody had spent a great deal of effort and money to put this road in. In this country, roads had been developed for one of two reasons: timber or mining. Other than a few scattered ponderosa pines, he recalled the timber as being scraggly. Some people called it piss-fir. He was sure loggers would not have put the road in, since most of the trees had little commercial value. Clicking with the mouse, he followed the road to the top where it branched into a pair of smaller two-track roads that disappeared into the thick timber. Both led into separate draws. He assumed, because of the nature of the drainage's name and the brightness of the vegetation, that there were springs in both of these draws. The place looked lush. In one draw, it looked like there could be a road-cut but the timber canopy and imagery shadows were too thick to get a good look at it. He zoomed back in, readjusted the aspect and studied the screen. There was a solid line in the vegetation that didn't look natural. It held promise. He put another "X" on the map.

Moving farther up the south divide, he looked hard at the East Fork. He knew the drainage well from patrols during elk season. In late October, he could always find a few hidden hunting camps tucked in the timbered draws but didn't recall signs of any mine shafts.

The East Fork drainage butted the upper West Fork and closed his circle. Again, Cove pondered the odds of a backcountry mine leaching toxins. He found himself mentally crossing his fingers. On horseback, it would take three or more days to cover it. And it was no place he was going to take his horses.

***

Cove headed down Main. At the highway, he turned left towards Morgan Creek and called Mendiola.

"You get lucky last night?" Mendiola asked, with a smile in his voice.

Cove came close to hanging up. He hadn't told Mendiola that he'd had drinks with Agent Duran.

"She wanted to talk about the foot." Cove sighed. "Your case."

"Sure, Charlie, that's what my wife and I talk about

when we go out. Sit down, order a drink, talk about amputated legs and shit."

"Look... you ever hunt the West Fork of Morgan Creek?"

"Is that where you're gonna take my kid huntin'?"

"No. Have you ever been in there?" Cove laid the question out as if he were beating a cowbell with a stick.

"I was thinking we might try up around Corkscrew."

"Fred... knock it off. Have you ever hunted the West Fork? Know of any old mines up there?"

"I don't think so. Hey, let me speak to Duran for a sec."

"Jesus, Fred." Cove didn't give him time to respond and hung up. He shook his head thinking about Mendiola. *Don't you have a dead body you need to find?*

He pulled off the road, let Annie out of the back and put her up front. She sat in the passenger side and looked at Cove. He needed some intelligence in his life.

Cove's phone buzzed. It was Mendiola. He brought it up to his ear.

"You done with the bullshit?" Cove asked.

"Sorry about that," Mendiola said. "This case's been bugging the crap out of me, and I need some humor, and you're it... This thing doesn't belong here. It oughta be in some toilet like San Diego. Somewhere on the border, not up here. I can't buy a burger without somebody asking me about the foot. I told the EMTs to keep their mouths shut, but that was a waste of breath. The commissioners keep asking. Hell, my wife asked me about it a couple of days ago. She never does that. Thank God the cartel angle hasn't slipped out into rumorville yet."

"I was thinking the same thing last night."

"You should be thinking of Duran. All bullshitting aside."

"I am thinking about her. I think she saved my bacon with your asshole ISP detective. Speaking of which, has he got any investigative direction on this thing? Is he chasing any leads at all, or is he still mumbling about me? I've got this sense that his dumb ass hit a wall."

"McGee's got the Visa that Rodriguez used to rent the truck. Talavera's. He's running all the purchases with it. Hopefully it'll show a trail. He rented the motel here using cash so I don't know. What I'm wondering is... did he stay in the room? Hell, maybe it's his alibi? For all I know, he rented it, and it was used by one of his buddies or never used. I should have asked the maid if the bed had been slept in. I started wondering about that when you figured out somebody else rented the room for him in Idaho Falls. There's obviously at least two of these fuckheads running around."

"Two?" Cove asked.

"Yeah. Rodriguez and the guy pushing the wheelchair."

Cove chewed his lip for a moment and let it go. "I assume he's chasing down the cell records, too?" Cove asked.

"McGee? No. Rodriguez didn't have a phone," Mendiola said.

Cove's head canted. It didn't make sense. "Everybody's got a cell phone. He had to have one."

"Jenks may be a farm boy, but when it comes to going through shit, he's anal. He milked that truck search for an hour in the Quonset hut. I finally had to tell him to go serve papers. He was gonna pull the door panels off. He's got something about tools."

The mention of the truck took Cove's memory back to the stump sticking out of the boot with the two severed leg bones and the call that Armando had gotten from Mexico. "Who in your office knows about the cartel's involvement?"

"Nobody. I was toying with briefing the Mackay and Stanley deputies, but I'm not gonna. Between you and me, I haven't told Jenks. Sure as shit, he'll tell his wife, and it'll be all over the county. CNN finds out about a chainsawed foot and looking for a cartel asshole, they'll be camped in the parking lot. Speaking of which, I got a call from Julie this morning. She wanted to know about the foot. She said somebody gave her a tip."

"Yeah, she called me. I told her to call you. She didn't get it from me."

"Two weeks ago, she said you weren't answering her calls."

Cove inhaled. "Is she going to write it?"

"I asked her to hold off," Mendiola said. "If it hits the papers, it's not going to help. Promised I'd give her the scoop if we made an arrest or found a body... Charlie, you oughta take a few days off, and go chase her around Boise."

Cove rubbed his leg. "Speaking of your missing dead man, Duran told me the pathologist concluded the foot was removed postmortem. I thought the same thing. What's Erdos's take on this? Depending on the credit card history McGee comes up with, you can more or less put Rodriguez in the county during the time the foot was amputated. Is he talking about issuing a John Doe death certificate?"

"Erdos? I'll talk to him when we've got a body. He's still sitting on Terzi's cert. It's been six months. I got a call from Terzi's sister a week ago. She's all pissed off. Claims she has a life insurance policy on him and can't file until there's a death certificate. Who the fuck carries life insurance on a meth head? I think it's probably bullshit... For some stupid reason, I promised to call Erdos. He said he's waiting on me to find the body. Wants an autopsy. Waiting on me, for shit's sake. Hell, an autopsy will cost the county two grand after x-ray and tox. Christ, it's no mystery how he died."

Cove's face flushed. He knew there were four options that the coroner could put down for the manner of death on a certificate—if it could be determined. They were suicide, accidental, natural, or homicide. The last bothered him, and he didn't understand why. The determination of manner of death would depend on the facts preceding Terzi's last moments and what an autopsy discovered—that was assuming there was a body to recover. He didn't believe anyone could conclude that it was a natural death but a suicide wasn't too big of a stretch. It would depend on why he'd chosen to go in the river. It could be an accidental death from drowning. If he'd bled to death, or drowned due to blood loss, *it was a homicide*. He wanted to ask Mendiola what he thought was so damn clear about Terzi's death. What *he* thought the manner of death was. But he wasn't sure he wanted the answer. And that was assuming Terzi was dead because it didn't feel like he'd killed him.

Chapter 14

On the highway, Cove passed the broken fence where Rodriguez had wrecked. His mind flashed back to the fact that they hadn't located a cell phone in the truck. It made no sense. If Rodriguez was truly a member of a Mexican drug cartel, he'd have to have some way of communicating with his superiors. He had to have a phone. *Everybody* had a phone. After a half-mile, he turned around. If the phone wasn't in the truck, it had to be in the field.

Cove pulled off the highway and let Annie out of the truck's bed. The two walked over to the broken fence post, and Cove watched curiously as Annie sniffed the spot where the boot had been found. She was interested but didn't perform an "alert" by sitting down. He wasn't surprised. She was trained to locate hidden carcasses, game meat, fish, firearms and spent shell casings. Human body parts were not part of her game. But she was curious.

Cove looked out at the spot where the Ford had come to rest. There were three chunks of ground that had been torn up while the vehicle was flipping end for end. There was a brown spot in the alfalfa, presumably from leaking fluids, where the vehicle had stopped. He looked back at the highway and envisioned Rodriguez over-correcting, the truck catching the edge of the pavement, skipping over the barrow-pit, contacting the ground at the fence line and then doing its three near-fatal flips. From the edge of the pavement to where the truck had stopped was about eighty yards and consisted of a straight line.

Cove turned to his dog, snapped a 30' leash on her and said, "Annie, let's get to work." He motioned the dog forward with his hand. He watched her work and fed her leash as she needed it. There was a breeze coming from the south, and Annie began cutting diagonally across its current. Her ears were up, and her nose kept working the air. Her tail was flipping back and forth. When Annie would reach the margin of the truck's path, Cove would tap the leash. She'd change direction, and the two would move farther up the scene. Ten yards after the first divot, Annie switched from scenting the air to sniffing in the vegetation. She suddenly wheeled about, sat down and stared at Cove expectantly. Cove was surprised. He didn't think there would be anything that would cause her to alert. He was expecting to see her gain interest in some unseen object in the alfalfa and that he would have to check out the spot and see what had caught her nose.

Cove walked over and kneeled. He took his hands and pushed the green stems away from where she had stuck her nose before she planted her butt. There was a spent silver-colored pistol shell casing caught in the vegetation. He looked at Annie. "Good girl!" he said and rubbed her head.

He photographed the cartridge in the vegetation and then picked it up by inserting his pen in the case's mouth. He brought it to his nose and smelled its faint smoky odor. It wasn't fresh, but there was still enough odor to conclude it had been fired within the last few weeks. It was a nickel-plated brass shell casing. The base was stamped with .45 AUTO R-P. What caught Cove's eye was the impression on the primer's face on the base of the case. Primers were made of soft malleable metal in order to take the hit from the firing pin and not allow the hot gasses to escape when the cartridge was fired. It was marked with a rectangular box. Vertical milling marks from the breech face of the gun that had fired it had been impressed parallel to the box. Inside the box was the flat mark where the firing pin had struck the primer. He'd seen this firing pin signature many times. Every other firearm he'd seen used a round firing pin. The gun that had fired this shell had a flat firing pin. There was no question in Cove's mind; the cartridge had been fired in a Glock pistol.

He pulled a Ziploc bag out of his pant pocket and dropped the casing into it. The find brought two questions to Cove. The first was, where was the pistol? But more curiously, why had there been a fired casing inside Rodriquez's truck? After a bit, he came up with two theories for the latter. Either the gun had been fired inside the truck or somebody had picked up a casing and put it in the vehicle. The gun could still be laying in the alfalfa.

He put Annie back to work with a flick of his hand. On her first transverse across the area, she stuck her nose in the alfalfa and paused before she moved on. Cove checked the spot. A can of Red Bull was smashed into the ground. They moved on. Annie became interested in another spot, and Cove moved his boot across the spot. There were several pieces of broken glass the size of gravel. Some of it was hung up in the vegetation, and some was on the ground. Cove was about to dismiss the spot when he saw something black. He kneeled down and parted the stalks with his hand. His pulse quickened. It was a folding cell phone. Collecting it with the baggie, he noticed a late model sedan had pulled in and parked across the highway from his truck. The windows were rolled up and he couldn't see the occupants. Cove assumed he was being watched out of curiosity and continued the search. By the time he got to where the inverted truck had been, they located another empty Red Bull can, a half-pack of Marlboro cigarettes, lots of broken glass and a side mirror. He ran Annie over the scene one more time, working back towards the highway. The car was still parked across the highway. The vehicle was beginning to bother him. He expected it to drive off when he got to his truck, but it stayed put. The driver's window was now cracked but still up. He kept the contents of the Ziploc hidden in his hand. After he loaded Annie, the sedan's window came all the way down, and he watched as the sunlight caught the short blonde hair of Renee Duran.

"Jesus, Duran," Cove said. "I was wondering who was eyeballing me."

"I swear I wasn't," Duran said and smiled. "I would have stepped out, but I didn't want to burn my car. Jump in. Show me what you found."

Cove walked around her car and got in the passenger side. The interior smelled like cinnamon.

"Just met with my informant," Duran said. "She hasn't heard anything about a Mexican running crystal. In fact, she thinks shit is scarce right now. I'll drive north and hit the Bitterroot tomorrow."

He handed her the Ziploc.

Duran's eyes widened. "A burner phone. Cool. These pricks'll sometimes carry two. A contract phone for family and a burner for their dirty work. They change the burners every few months. Especially after we took down the Narco Polo case." Duran noticed the fired pistol case. "Interesting on the shell."

I just wonder where the gun is," Cove said. "It's out of a Glock. I'm sure it's not in the field. Annie would have found it."

"If it was used to kill the guy who had his foot cut off, it's probably in the river."

Duran handed the evidence bag back to Cove. "I assume you're going to sign this over to Fred?"

Cove nodded. "Yeah, not my case."

"He'll turn the phone over to me or McGee. If he gives it to McGee, his boss will make him turn it over to us. This case is way bigger than Idaho. The weasel will drag his feet. It'll turn into a bureaucratic multi-agency goat screw." She widened her eyes. "It'll take three weeks, maybe a month before I see it. Some of the numbers will get stale."

"I assume you've got a chain-of-evidence sheet?" Cove asked.

She nodded.

"It's yours. I'll give the .45 case to Fred."

"I owe you a steak dinner," Duran said. "The incoming and outgoing numbers on this thing could be a glory-hole. We've got plenty of PC on Rodriguez for wiretaps on all these numbers with his history." She nodded and looked out the windshield. "The fact he can't be in the country, and the severed foot...Talavera..." She sounded as if she was talking to herself. "The judge'll give us two weeks to run the tap unless we come up with something solid. It'll produce if we jump on it. Probably a lot." She frowned and looked at Cove. "What're you going to tell Fred?"

He shrugged. "The truth."

***

Cove turned his truck around and headed for Mendiola's office. The sheriff was sitting at his desk, talking on the phone. Cove sat down and set an evidence envelope on the desk. Mendiola hung up.

"Jenks says he can't do his shift. Irritable bowel syndrome. Maybe you oughtta run for sheriff."

"It's a .45 case fired out of a Glock. Annie found it and a cell phone at the crash site. I turned the phone over to Duran."

Mendiola's wrinkles looked older. "Jenks thinks dogs are for chasing cows." He opened the envelope and looked at the casing for a moment. "McGee'll want me to arrest you for obstructing or some such thing." He looked at Cove and smiled. "He's gonna shit blood when he hears about the phone."

"He carries a .45 Glock." Cove said. "Ask him where he was that night." Cove canted his head. "Maybe I planted it."

"Jenks found one in Rodriquez's truck too."

Cove's head turned. Two fired casings had been in the truck, along with a dead man's foot. He blinked and after a moment, he asked, "Is the truck still in the Quonset?"

"Yeah, I'm keeping it until this case is closed or I retire."

Cove looked at him. "Can I take a peek at it?"

***

The Quonset hut was cool, dark and dusty. Mendiola turned the building's fluorescent lights on. The truck was upright. It was a silver four-door F150 that leaned a bit because the driver's side tires had been pulled off their rims during the crash. The driver's door had been cut off with a pneumatic extraction tool and was leaning upright in the truck's bed. The passenger's side and rear doors had been forced open. The windshield was shattered. The side and rear windows were gone. The front of the roof was bent partway down. Dark dirt was smeared on the hood and driver's side along with green scuffs of alfalfa.

Cove looked inside. It smelled of cigarette smoke. A bloody airbag hung limply from the steering wheel. The rearview mirror was hanging from a cable. He pulled his SureFire light off his belt and shined it inside. Thumb-sized bits of broken glass were scattered throughout the truck. Dried blood was smeared on the ceiling where Jenks had found Rodriguez in the inverted cab.

"Poke around," Mendiola said. "I've gotta make some calls."

Cove thought about the two shell casings. The theory that made the most sense was that the Glock had been fired inside the vehicle and the shells had been ejected just before the gun's slide had chambered the next round. He'd seen this many times with poachers.

Cove looked at the front charcoal-colored fabric seats. A console sat between them. He could see what appeared to be dried blood on three surfaces. A smear on the driver's seat, a second smear on the console and a spot the size of a small pancake on the passenger's seat. This round dark spot jumped at him. He thought about the truck tumbling over and ending up on its top. He let the video play in slow motion in his head. He saw the windows shatter, and he watched Rodriguez's loose body bounce violently around the cab. Cove's head canted, and he watched it again. He could see no way that the spot on the passenger's seat had come from Rodriguez. Not during or after the crash. It had to come from a source that was on the seat when the truck was upright. Gravity only worked one way.

He shined his light on the ceiling. There'd been pooled blood above the driver's seat that had run towards the driver's door. Cove assumed this had taken place when the wrecker driver rolled the vehicle upright and after the EMTs had extracted Rodriguez. He walked around to the passenger's side and slowly worked his light, focusing on the vertical surfaces. His pulse quickened. On the right side of the console, he found a small half-round pattern of blood spatter. The oval drops of blood were about the size of grape seeds. Other than a hand-sized smear, he found none on the dashboard. Two small drops had hit the passenger's side of the rearview mirror and he found several more drops on the right side of the steering column. He studied the passenger door and post and found no blood. He stepped back to the truck's bed and shined his light on the driver's door. Nothing caught his attention. He let the crash video run again in his mind. This time he ran it in slow motion, looking for some way that would explain these spatter patterns. Nothing clicked.

Game warden work was frequently bloody. Cove had no formal training on blood spatter analysis. However, he'd read about the science and had used the interpretation techniques on wildlife cases. He'd observed lots of blood in the back of pickups, on the clothes and boots of hunters. There'd been many a campsite where he'd found drips of blood under an empty meat pole. He'd checked hunters who claimed they hadn't killed anything and then handed him their license with fingernails edged with dried blood. He'd seen where bullets had left spatter in the snow that looked like a red mist after the projectile had exited an animal. He'd found drips of blood on rocks that told him what direction the animal had been moving. And he'd seen blowback on his face and shirt after crawling under a downed tree to euthanize a road-crippled deer.

Significantly, he believed that the blood in the truck came from two sources. Most of it was from Rodriguez as he tumbled around the truck during the crash and had laid on the upended ceiling. But the round spot on the passenger's seat and the spatter was a different deal. He supposed the spatter could have come from arterial bleeding. He'd never seen that type of spatter, but he thought it would look different, more linear than the shotgun pattern of blowback.

Assuming that the DNA from the spatter and the seat spot were the same, he couldn't come up with any other explanation. He suspected–based on the shell casings, the spatter, the bloody seat and who was driving the truck—that someone had been shot while sitting in the passenger's seat and that the bullet or bullets had failed to exit the body. The shots had come from the driver's seat or possibly through the open window; the projectiles had struck the passenger's body, causing the blowback spatter.

He walked out of the Quonset hut. The sun exposed dirt on his green Levi's from leaning against the bed of the truck. He brushed the dirt off and went back into Mendiola's office.

The sheriff had a black land-line phone handset clamped to his ear and was listening. He rolled his eyes. Cove grabbed his coffee mug from the back room, filled it up and sat down in front of the sheriff.

Mendiola hung up the phone. "That was your buddy. I was right. He's shittin' blood. Started ranting about you and the phone. Asked me if you're sleeping with Duran. Told him that as near as I could tell, Indians didn't get laid."

Cove's eyes rolled. "Is he working on the shell case that Jenks recovered?"

"No. I told him about it the day we found it. He said there was no reason, since we didn't have a gun or a body." Mendiola had a thick manila folder in front of him. Rodriguez's name written on its tab.

Cove motioned to the file. "In the photo with Talavera's body, there's two yellow evidence markers. Did they find shell casings?"

Mendiola's hand came up to his ear, and his eyes looked down at the case folder. "Good question." He licked his lower lip and nodded. He dug the photo out of the file and studied the tent-like markers. "Can't see any in this. If they did," he sounded like he was talking to himself, "and it matches the one Jenks found, I think I see enough for a murder warrant down there." Mendiola rubbed his cheeks. "Hell yes, there's more than enough."

Cove nodded. "Did Jenks say Rodriguez had arterial bleeding?"

Mendiola shook his head His eyes came up. "No. Why?"

"There's blood in the truck that I don't believe is from the accident. Some of it's spatter. There's a spot on the passenger seat that doesn't make any sense, and there's some spots that look like blowback." Cove massaged his thigh. "Like somebody got shot while they were sitting there."

"You shittin' me?" Mendiola asked and stood up.

"No," Cove said and followed him out the door. "I'm not. It would be interesting to compare the DNA of the blood to the foot."

Cove showed him the seat and the spatter patterns. The sheriff took Cove's flashlight and studied the truck for several minutes.

Mendiola pointed the light at the stain on the seat. "Assuming this ain't spilled salsa, I see what you're talking about. I can't say about the spatter. A guy bouncing inside a rolling truck's gonna make a mess." Fred looked at Cove. "Are we sure this isn't something else? Something spilled?"

"Let me grab a strip."

Cove returned from his truck with a white plastic bottle and a water container. "I've had too many guys try to bullshit me about drops of ketchup on their tailgates. Apparently, they don't watch much TV."

Cove pulled a thin white piece of paper out of the bottle. One end was painted with a yellow substance. He moistened the tip, touched it to the seat stain for a moment and then turned it over. The yellow had turned green.

Cove showed Mendiola and shrugged. "Blood."

"I'll talk to McGee's boss. He can get somebody who does blood at the lab. I know they've got somebody who does that stuff."

Cove brushed his pants off again and looked at his hands. Something wasn't right.

Chapter 15

Cove turned onto the West Fork road, stopped and looked up at the drainage. It was steeper than the view from Google Earth. On the south side, the timber looked lush and shadowy and held the promise of elk. On the north side, it was high desert that looked into the sun. It was covered by sagebrush that never seemed to get taller than your ankle and bunch grass that was beginning to blanche from the heat of summer. It was a place to look for the white rumps of antelope. Cove could see the two-track that ran up the dry ridge. It looked like two pale parallel cords threading through the sage. Other than this morning's tour on Google Earth, he'd never been on the road, but he now knew why it was there.

The color of the hillside caused him to pause. It was the same color of the dirt that had rubbed off onto his pants. When he'd passed the crash site, he'd noticed that the wreck had exposed a black loamy soil. It was soil that had been cultivated for a hundred years. Most of the dirt on the exterior of the truck had come from the field. The dirt on his pants had come from the truck's fender and exhaust pipe. It was light-colored. He thought about the soil color from around Challis. The hills around the town were a reddish color. In front of Armando's trailer was this same chalky-colored stuff. He thought about where Rodriguez's truck had come from and the dirt in the photo with Talavera's lipless body lying in the desert. He recalled that the dirt looked almost pink.

He stepped out of his truck and looked at the dried mud that caked its fenders and exhaust pipe, and compared it to the dirt that was still on his uniform pants. It was the same color.

He thought about Duran's hypothesis. She believed that Rodriguez had killed Talavera, rented the truck using his stolen credit card and driver's license and had delivered the severed lips to an unknown location. He had then headed to Idaho or maybe Montana, had killed someone else and removed a foot with a chainsaw and had been headed south to deliver it to an unknown subject. She also believed he had disposed of the gun, probably in the river. *Had he dumped the chainsaw in the river too?* Cove hadn't thought about where one might use a chainsaw to remove a dead person's foot until now. *He didn't do it in somebody's back yard. He did it in the hills.* After a moment, he shook his head. The Rodriguez case wasn't his, and it had distracted him from what he needed to focus on. It was time to get back to work.

He had two choices, either go up and look at the mine, or look in the draw below it for water that made its way down the otherwise dry face into the West Fork. No matter what was going on at the mine shaft, the bottom line was whether or not it was polluting the creek. With that in mind, he headed up the bottom of the West Fork.

As he drove along the road, he studied the creek

through the breaks in the willows. Nothing caught his eye. When he got to the draw that held the mine, he stopped and studied its bone dry course through the passenger window. It didn't look like it had run water since snowmelt. He got out and looked at the vegetation in it. The brush was higher than on the side hills. Rock pillars framed the sides of the draw. Where it met the road, a galvanized culvert jutted from the road bed. Cove studied it for a moment, and the skin on his neck prickled up. He grabbed a small rock and lobbed it towards the culvert. It rang like a broken bell. Nothing buzzed inside it. He eased over to it, thinking about a potential pissed-off rattlesnake. The mouth of the pipe brought back the hunt for Terzi, and he took a deep breath.

A soft chirruping came from the draw above him. He shaded his eyes and looked for the bluebird. A bit of dusky-blue movement caught his eye in the sagebrush. Thinking about the mine farther up, he wondered whose it had been and what he'd found. Most of the holes these men had dug had held empty promises.

Cove was an early American history reader. His office in his room had shelves of books that covered the 1800s and the so-called taming of the west. Lone men had choked this country after the Civil War. He'd seen the remains of their dirt-roofed cabins dug into the hillsides. They were just big enough for one man. They'd walked these creeks carrying a shovel and a gold pan and claimed they were looking for riches, but Cove believed they were looking for something else. These loaners had seen lots of good men die. They'd seen piles of amputated arms and legs and had heard the moans. He knew they were haunted by their own dreams. These runaways poked and scraped at the alluvials lying in the creek beds and up the side gullies, while trying to put their nightmares in the past. They'd wash the gravel in their pans, looking for a line of bright color on the edge of black sand, sampling each creek and draw. It was called prospecting. They weren't trying to make a living off the gold they found in their pans; they were looking for the mother lode, the source of the metal washed by the floods of time. He believed they were searching for a place to dig a hole.

Cove crossed the road and walked to the creek. He sat down on a cottonwood log and studied the water. The air was cooler, and the water gurgling over the dark rocks cleared his mind. Had this not been the West Fork, he would have let Annie out to refresh herself. It looked fresh and drinkable. He wondered if there were any fish in it.

A loud-hollow tapping caught his ear from downstream. The noise shifted to the flapping of wings and a rapid series of high-pitched rhythmic tones that could have been made by an acoustic guitar. Cove caught a glimpse of its red head and black and white markings on its broad wings before it disappeared into the leaves of a cottonwood.

A stonefly landed on his knee. Its shape and coloration were as striking as the pileated woodpecker he'd just seen. It was about as long as his thumb was wide and was the burnished gold of a balsam-root flower. Its translucent lace-like wings were folded flat over its carapace and extended almost to the tip of its segmented abdomen. Six articulated legs gripped the cloth of Cove's pant leg. The insect's twin antennae moved left and right as if they were the staffs of a blind man feeling the darkness, but these organs were listening and tasting the air. It pivoted and faced Cove. The creature's black eyes appeared to be staring into his. It was if the bug was curious or had an intellect. The skin on Cove's neck tingled. It was the same feeling he'd had when he'd heard the owl calling after sunrise in Gooseberry.

If the insect was truly studying Cove, it could see that the human's head was frozen, and his torso was as unflinching as the rocky walls behind him. The man's brown eyes were focused on the essence of this slender golden fly. His brain was on fire; this was an *aquatic insect*. It shouldn't be alive in these waters. Its egg had been deposited on the surface of the creek a year ago. It had lived in the water until last night when it had crawled out and shed its skin, morphing into a winged creature that had but a day or two to lay its eggs and die. What Cove couldn't understand was how it had survived the toxins that had killed the fish and the mergansers and god knows what else. Looking upstream, he saw a second golden stonefly flittering across an eddy behind a water-polished rock. He gently nudged the insect off his leg, and it took flight.

Cove stepped to the edge of the creek, reached in and pulled out a brick-colored rock the size of a flattened soft ball. He turned it over. It was crawling with life. Dark mayfly nymphs skittered about, trying to find a crack or some other refuge. Several caddis larvae clung to its surface, their bodies protected by armored cases. He felt like he'd found something more precious than shiny flakes of metal in a gold pan.

Cove was three quarters of a mile from where he'd found the nearest dead fish. It was time to do his own prospecting. He got back in his truck, turned around and drove down to the bridge that crossed over the West Fork. It was where he'd found the first merganser. He walked down to the creek and picked up a fist-sized rock and turned it over. Nothing. He picked up a second one and still nothing. No insects. He notice that neither of these felt slick like the rocks above. He realized that the slickness had been from a thin layer of algae that was growing on the rocks upstream. This water was dead. The water above was full of life.

He got back in his truck and drove half way to the gulch, found an opening in the brush and trotted to the creek. A quick sampling produced no sign of life. He jumped back in his truck and cut the distance to the gulch in half again. Before he rolled the rock over, he could feel the life on its surface. It was slick. The bottom of it was crawling with bugs. He turned and looked down the drainage. The source of whatever was killing everything in the creek was within a quarter of a mile. There were no side creeks entering from the north, but two hundred yards below him was a steep timbered draw on the south side. It was Fourth Spring Creek. Just above its confluence, he sampled and found the rocks covered with life. He dropped below the creek and felt the rocks in the water. They were clean. He pulled one out and confirmed there were no aquatic insects living under it.

Cove looked up Fourth Spring Creek. The tributary tumbled down a steep rocky cut in an arc and disappeared behind a point of rocks. It was shadowed by conifers, mostly Doug fir with a few ponderosa pines. The stream was about three paces wide and maybe a foot deep. What struck Cove was that it was a creek he'd normally have taken a drink out of.

He felt like he'd found his mother lode. Or at least the drainage where it was hidden.

Cove parked his truck in a cluster of cottonwoods next to the West Fork. He let Annie out and motioned with his hand towards the creek bed upstream from Fourth Spring Creek. She walked in, laid down in the stream and lapped. He pulled out a hydration pack from the cab and locked it up. He wished he'd left Annie home. It was going to be a challenge to keep her from drinking, but it was doable as long as he kept her on a heel and shared his water.

He found a spot where a cottonwood had fallen, and using it and an exposed rock, he managed to get cross the West Fork without getting wet. Climbing uphill, he found it easiest to follow the creek a few yards outside the thick brush of the riparian zone. The hillside smelled fresher than the bottom of the creek. It had a scent made from tall conifers, hunks of red bark and downed trees that were slowly turning into soil. Underneath the canopy of each fir and pine tree, the ground was covered with circles of brown needles. Outside the duff-rings were thick patches of bright-green bunch grasses. In the deep shade, there were patches of moist green moss. On the north side of the older trees, shelf fungi clung to the bark. Old man's moss hung from their lower branches. It was a place he could envision his grandmother collecting leaves and roots for her medicinal collection. It was the polar opposite of the south facing slope across the West Fork.

He moved up the slope with Annie at his heel. A deep "kraa-kraa" came from a raven somewhere on the mountainside above him. Cove stopped and listened. The song of the creek ran down the hill. A guttural bell-like noise came from farther away. He wasn't sure if it was a second raven or the first one moving off. It conjured up the image of his grandfather talking about a raven from long ago. He tried to recall the tale, but all that he could remember was the old man telling him to only repeat the story on long nights when the snow was on the ground.

Cove looked at Annie. Her ears were up, and her nostrils were moving air in and out. She was looking in the direction from where the first raven call had called. He stood still for a minute, perhaps two, listening and trying to catch what she was smelling.

He eased up the hill, watching where he placed his boots, studying the ground for sticks and rocks that if stepped on could give up his location. Slowing his pace, he steadied his breathing so he could listen while he moved. Other than the creek's music, the hillside was quiet. The silence caught his attention. There was something missing. Not a chickadee or a song-sparrow. This was a north slope Doug fir community carved by a willowed creek. It was thick with habitat. The place should be alive with life. Again, he studied Annie and watched her nostrils flex.

Some forty yards farther, the breeze brought the sour odor to his nose. Moving a few more feet, the source came into view. It was a doe mule deer lying dead under a fir. There were long arcs in the needles where her legs had flailed during her last minutes. Her head and neck were arched backwards. It was clear the animal had not died quietly. It hadn't laid down and curled up like they did in the winter. It had been a violent struggle, and yet he could see no blood or wound.

Cove pulled his iPhone from his pocket and took a photo of the doe. He thought about what could have caused her death. If she had been shot and wounded, she would have run downhill and probably would have died in the creek bottom. Poachers usually stuck to the roads so they could quickly get in and out of the area, but this doe seemed too far from a road for that theory. If it had been a mountain lion, he would have expected the animal to have been buried under pine needles and branches, and its cervical vertebrae would have been crushed by the cat's jaws. A wolf would have chased it to the bottom of the West Fork and drug it down by its flank. And any predator would have fed on it.

He took the doe's front legs and rolled her over. He saw the green tinge of decomposition on her belly. There was no dark stain in the pine needles and no obvious wounds on the animal's back side. Flexing the legs, he concluded that rigor mortis had come and gone. He examined her eyes and found them sunken from dehydration. Her ears were still soft and her belly was slightly bloated. Flies had laid their eggs in her mouth. A few of the tiny larvae had hatched. He added everything up, and he figured that she had been dead for two days at the most. He ran his hands against the grain of her hair, making sure there wasn't a bullet hole he'd missed.

He stood up and looked at her. The most telling evidence was the marks in the duff where her legs had arced back and forth. It was as if she'd had a seizure just before she died. Cove wondered if a brain condition had cursed the doe's death. An aneurysm or maybe a tumor. He'd read about a parasite that infected the brains of moose, but he'd never heard of the disease in mule deer, and he'd never heard of it in Idaho. With moose, it caused them to walk in circles, but he didn't know if they had convulsions. There was also the possibility that it was chronic wasting disease, but that sickness hadn't been documented in Idaho either. He looked over at Fourth Spring Creek. It was about sixty yards off, and the doe was facing away from it. It was conceivable that she'd drank from it and walked over and died. *Was there arsenic in the water from a mine above him? Did arsenic poisoning cause convulsions?*

Cove walked over to the creek. He flashed Annie his open palm, and she sat down on her haunches and watched him with her ears cocked.

Studying the moist soil along the bank, he found two sets of deer tracks. They were the tracks of a doe and fawn. *The doe drank, and maybe the fawn didn't because it's nursing.*

He let Annie drink from his hydration pack, and the two headed back towards the doe. Cove moved his arm ahead and said, "Okay." Annie broke from his side and started working ahead of him as if the two were bird hunting. But they weren't–they were looking for a fawn. The two made a broad half circle around the doe without finding anything. Cove was surprised by the buzz from his phone. He pulled it out of his shirt pocket. It was a text message from his boss. This was a huge curiosity. He'd never gotten a text message from George. The guy had cursed text messages. He opened it up: "Dax got his ass kicked."

Cove stared at the phone, rubbed the back of his neck and wondered what George had meant by "ass kicked." He selected Dax's number and brought the phone to his ear. While he waited for it to connect, he thought about the message. It could mean that Dax Sparks had been assaulted, or it could mean that some butthead had caught a salmon and had managed to speed off with the fish before Dax could get to him. *Had somebody jumped Dax? Was he okay?*

The phone never rang. Cove checked the connection and wasn't surprised that he'd lost cell coverage. What wasn't a mystery was that George had expected him to work the Holman hole with Sparks and that he was in trouble.

Chapter 16

Cove called Dax Spark's phone twice before he hit the highway. Both times it went directly to voice mail. Either the phone wasn't in an area with cell service, he was using the phone, or it was turned off. He'd called Spark's land line and got his answering machine. Twice he'd found George's name in his phone's contacts and he'd almost pushed the connect button, but he wanted to find out what had happened to Dax, and what Dax had told their boss.

The other thing that was bothering him was that Bob Johnson had called and left him a phone message: "Charlie, the lab says the water sample is clean. Call me." The news was befuddling. The only theory that had made any sense to Cove was the leaching of acid and arsenic from an old mine.

Cove liked being a game warden. He considered it a job that reflected the Salish ties to the earth. A connection he wanted. It was a job he believed his grandfather would have approved of, perhaps even honored, if he'd had the time to understand what it was about—despite his hatred of game wardens that had come from the Swan River murders.

Part of why Cove enjoyed his job was that he seemed to be able to understand the problems that developed in his patrol area and put them into boxes. Categorize them. Develop theories. But what was happening on the West Fork didn't fit a box. Dead fish, dead mergansers and now this dead doe didn't make any sense. It didn't fit a box he could understand.

As he approached Challis, he glanced over at the clinic. There were two Fish and Game trucks parked in front of it. One was Dax Spark's and the other was George Nayman's.

When he entered the building, the receptionist was on the phone. She nodded towards the back and mouthed, "They're back there."

Nayman and Sparks were standing over a gurney with their backs towards him. A man was laying on it and had one wrist handcuffed to its frame. A female dressed in green scrubs was suturing the guy's face. She looked up at Cove, and the two wardens turned around. Dax's shirt was covered with blood and he had a bandage across the base of his nose. Bloody gauze hung out of his nostrils. Despite the mess, he was grinning like a kid with a mouthful of gumdrops.

Nayman was wearing a deep frown. "Look who decided to join the living. Where the hell you been?" His bald scalp was as red as a tomato, and the color seemed to ooze through the gray hair on the sides of his head.

George's eyes were drilling into Cove's. Charlie turned back to Dax. "What happened?"

"Dumb-ass thought he could take me," Sparks said, sounding like he had the cold from hell.

The man on the gurney tried to sit up. He was barrel-chested and had short hair. The nurse, or NP or whatever she was, pushed him back down. "You boys want to tell stories, take it outside."

"Watch your prisoner," Nayman said to Sparks. He and Cove walked past the receptionist and out the front door.

"Am I getting Alzheimer's, Charlie? Am I confused or didn't I tell you to show the kid how to work that hole?"

Cove studied his boss for a bit. "I figured it was a one-man deal. I always worked Holman by myself." Cove's head sunk a notch. "I guess it was a two-manner this morning."

For a moment, neither said anything. Finally George spoke, "He says it was his idea to work it alone." Nayman's eyes narrowed. "I expect to be bullshitted, but not by *the guys who work for me.*" George growled the last few words.

"It was me. My idea. Not his. This one's on me," Cove said. "It's this West Fork thing. I'm sorry. I found a dead deer in there this morning. I can't find a mark on it. There's no aquatics in that section of the creek. I would have loved to have gone up and worked the Holman hole with him, but there's something going on and I don't know what the hell it is."

"You skin it? I worked an elk case once that I couldn't find a bullet hole anywhere. Turned out he'd shot it right up the asshole."

"No. I didn't open it up." Cove pulled his phone out and showed George the photo he'd taken of the doe. She was lying on her side. Her neck was arched, and the duff had been scraped in wide semi-circles where her hooves had flailed. "I think she'd just drunk out of Fourth Spring Creek. It's a trib that dumps into the West Fork. All the bugs in the creek are dead below there, but there's plenty above it. You can feel algae on the rocks, but not below it."

George pulled a pair of reading glasses out of his shirt pocket and studied the photo. "There can't be that goddamned much poison coming out of a mine, can there?" George asked.

Cove shook his head and put the phone away. "Johnson left me a message while I was up on the hill. The lab said the water was fine. Said it was clean."

"Then this doe died of something else," George said. "It's gotta be a disease that killed those fish. This deer musta died of something else. Shit, Charlie, you spend enough time in the woods, you find dead critters. Things die."

Cove watched the old warden as he spoke. His gray eyes were crunched up as if he were puzzled; they wandered off and looked up to his right as if he were trying visualize what could have caused the deer's death.

"Let me call Johnson," Cove said. "I'm hoping he'll send a crew up and electroshock the West Fork. See if there's any fish left. Maybe it was a one-time deal." He hesitated and rolled his shoulders. "You want me to drop it and work the Holman hole with Dax, no problem."

The door to the clinic opened. The man who had been on the gurney came through followed by Dax Sparks. Cove recognized him as the short guy who had eyeballed him in the bar. His thick arms were handcuffed behind his back, and he was staring at the ground. The right side of his face was a rose-red bruise that started at his ear and stopped at the hollow of his nose. In the middle of the mess, there was a stitched-up laceration that was forked and looked like an inverted Y. The blood-soaked gauze still hung from Dax's nostrils.

"You guys go get him booked in," Nayman said, "I'm gonna go over to Pallid's office and grease the skids." He pulled Cove off to the side. "Put him in the box, and get him to talk about the fight. See what you can pull out of him. Find out if he's been fishing that hole before this morning, and what caused the blowup. Pallid'll try to dump this thing."

While Nayman drove off, Cove helped Sparks get his prisoner strapped into the passenger side of the truck. The man was passive and didn't speak.

"I tried to call," Cove said. "You got your phone turned off?"

Dax closed the truck's door and flashed Cove his shit-eating grin. He pulled a smart phone out of his shirt pocket and showed the screen to Cove. It was shattered and smeared with dried blood. "Don't ever blindside a man who's trying to talk on his phone."

***

"You want some coffee?" Cove asked.

The man glared for a moment and then nodded. Cove studied his dark eyes. They were unblinking and didn't flick about the room. He was wearing a jumpsuit that was splashed with alternating orange and white stripes. The stripes were as wide as a man's fist. His wrists were cuffed and shackled to a chain that was padlocked around his waist. The man's neck was wider than his head, and he looked like he could bench press a horse.

"Do we need to keep those cuffs on?" Cove asked.

The man hesitated, and Cove watched his face and hands. He knew what the answer was going to be, but it was his body's voice—not his words—that was going to determine if he risked removing them.

The man looked down at his jail slippers, his arms seemed to relax, he gave a muted head shake and said, "No."

Cove stepped back from the room and half closed the door. He found the jailer, asked her to remove the man's belly chains and flipped through the guy's booking folder. It was a short outline that focused on his physical description, drug and alcohol usage, current employment and medical and arrest histories. There were the usual front and side booking photos, a close-up of his injured face and a shot of Jesus on a crucifix tattooed on his muscular shoulder.

When Cove returned to the room, the man had moved his chair up to the table and had his arms crossed on his chest. The tendons on his forearms flexed like rope. Cove set the two coffee mugs down and took the chair across from him. "You go by Butch, don't you?"

"Yeah." The man said it with a deep growl.

"I'm Charlie Cove."

The man held a stone glare and didn't reply. Cove studied his bruised and cut face. His skin around his orbit was swelling and his eye was starting to close. As bruised as he looked, he didn't give off an aura of a beaten man. Cove wondered if removing the man's shackles had been a mistake. He had already given him a weapon. If the man was looking for another fight, it'd be nasty, and he had to get him settled down.

Cove thought about seeing this man walk into the bar. He'd come in wearing a silver rodeo buckle and walked as if he was pissed at somebody. "Weren't you in the Borah the other night? Sitting at the bar?"

He nodded, and the edges of his face broke into a leer. A vein pulsed on his forehead. "That dyke your girlfriend?"

"No, she's not. Didn't you used to rodeo?"

"What did you guys do with my truck?"

Cove hesitated. He'd used this room many times. It had the smell of old paint and a hum that made one pause. The back wall was shelved and covered with law books and three-ring binders. The other walls were bare, with the exception of a smoke detector that had been gutted to hide a camera and a microphone. It was formally called the interview room. Informally, it was referred to as "the box." Other than incidental meetings with sheriff staff, there were two types of conversations that took place in this room—calling them conversations was a stretch, since they frequently were so one-sided, they didn't fit the definition of the word. The judicial system split these talks into two camps: interviews and interrogations. Cove didn't know which one this event was going to fall into.

The table that Butch Wilson sat in front of was the centerpiece of the room. Its gray laminate surface was scratched with initials, obscene drawings and profanities. Twice, Cove had been on the wrong side of this cold table. Both times he'd been facing McGee.

What Cove wanted out of this mental wrestling match

was to get Clarence "Butch" Wilson to admit that he'd hit Dax first, and hopefully a second admission that the salmon that Sparks had watched him slip into his truck was not a one-time event. He recognized that an accusatory line of questioning wasn't going to work with a hostile cowboy.

"Before we get any further, I need to Mirandize you. You've got the right to remain silent. Anything you say, can and will be used––"

Wilson interrupted. "I know my rights. Where's my goddamned truck?"

"I suspect you do." Cove thought about the two previous arrests for battery he'd seen on his rap sheet and wondered who he had punched. "But right now, I'm on my boss's shit list. We both know how bosses can be. He's gonna ask. So bear with me for a sec... Anything you say, can and will be used against you. You've got the right to an attorney. If you can't afford one, one will be appointed." Cove looked at him and flared his eyes. "You understand?"

"Yeah. Where's my truck?"

Cove noticed that Wilson was gripping the coffee mug by wrapping his big hand around it. The fingers looked tight. He decided that if the guy swung the mug at him, he was going to roll the table over him before he could stand up. He didn't have a plan for what would happen after that.

Cove pulled three white pills out of his pocket and set them in front of the man. "Aspirin. Your truck will be at the wrecker's yard. There's nothing I can do about that." Cove took a sip of his coffee and thought for a moment. He needed a theme for this interview. Something tangential

184

that would sidetrack Wilson's hostilities. "This's some nasty shit they make in here." Cove set his mug on the table and looked into Wilson's eyes. "You really think she's a dyke?"

The man's head turned at an odd angle. "Kinda looks like it. Got that lesbo haircut." He threw the pills in his mouth and washed them down with coffee.

Cove squinted. "She was kinda ogling the bartender. You see the way they were looking at each other?"

"Lisa? She ain't no queer." The man's face relaxed, he unfolded his arms, laid them on the table with his palms open and smiled. "I can guarantee *that*."

Cove watched the man unwind and thought about bringing up the bartender's tattooed cleavage. "Sparks is a smart ass, isn't he?" The way Cove said it, it was more of a statement than a question.

"Little shit pissed me off."

"He pisses everybody off. That's why I say he's a smart ass." Cove nodded and leaned towards the man. His chair creaked on the linoleum floor. "He say something to you?"

"Kept calling me fuckin' Clarence. I gave him my driver's license and told him to call me Butch."

Cove's head canted. "He called you *fucking* Clarence?"

"No." He shook his head. "Just Clarence." The man sat back and folded his arms.

Cove mimicked his body language and nodded. "And then you busted him?"

"Knocked the shit out of him."

Cove's head bobbed and his lips twisted up. "Didn't look like you slapped him."

The man stuck his right hand out and flexed his wide

fingers. "Fuck no, look here."

There were open red contusions on three of his knuckles.

"How many times you hit him?" Cove asked.

"Once. Then the chickenshit smacked me with a fuckin' rock."

Cove shook his head and thought of Spark's broken iPhone. "No wonder you called him chickenshit." He took a sip of coffee. "He said he was talking on the phone. What the hell was that all about?"

"Callin' to see if I had a fishing license. Didn't believe me. Called me fuckin' Clarence again to whoever the fuck he was talking to. I smacked him."

"He said you'd caught a salmon."

The man nodded.

"Holman's a good hole," Cove said. "There shoulda been an open season this year. There's a lotta fish."

"No shit. What's it gonna cost to get my truck?"

"Bait or a spinner?"

"Eggs."

"Salmon or steelhead?" Cove asked.

"Salmon eggs."

"You buy 'em?"

"I cure 'em myself. Store-bought ain't as good. My wife's gonna shit. What's it gonna cost to get it back?"

"You borax 'em?" Cove asked.

"Yeah, that and some cherry Jell-O. I think the color helps. I use a big glob of 'em. They stay on the hook good."

"You really think she's a dyke?" Cove asked.

The guy wrinkled up his face and gave Cove a curious look. "Shit, I don't know."

"You get those salmon eggs out of a hen you caught in there?"

"Yeah–" The man stopped, looked at Cove and then he hunched up and frowned. "Kiss my ass. Go ask my fuckin' attorney."

***

Cove stepped out of the room and spoke to the jailer. "He's all yours, but do me a favor and photograph his knuckles." He turned to George and Dax. "Let's step outside."

It wasn't a full confession. More of an admission. But Cove had gotten what he wanted out of Butch Wilson– mostly. He'd admitted to striking Sparks while he'd be on the phone. It was enough evidence that Wilson would probably enter a guilty plea to battery on a peace officer.

Dax had gotten rid of his bloody uniform shirt and was wearing a gray t-shirt with a Fish and Game logo screened over the pocket. The bloody gauze was gone from his nose. Two dark bruises were beginning to show under his eyes. Cove studied his face and concluded the pain was beginning to get to him.

He turned to Nayman. "Pallid buy off on the felony?"

"Says it's weak. Said the guy'll claim self-defense. Said he'll claim Dax hit him first."

Dax blurted, "What?"

Cove shook his head. "He admitted punching you first. Said you kept calling him fucking Clarence." Cove smiled. "He thinks you're chickenshit." He turned back to his boss. "Started to admit to catching another salmon and then lawyered up. Not enough for a search warrant."

Nayman turned to Sparks. "Pallid will want to dump one of the two counts in a plea. You need to figure out which one can walk. The assault or the salmon?"

Cove heard a vehicle enter the parking lot. He turned and saw Mendiola's Ford Excursion stop in front of the office. It was white with blue and red graphics. The word "Sheriff" was emblazoned over a seven-point gold star on the door.

Mendiola stepped out and turned to Cove. "When you get a sec, come on in."

The passenger was coroner Dave Erdos.

When Cove stepped back into the building, he found Mendiola sitting behind his desk. Erdos was sitting across from him, looking at an open manila file folder. He was in his sixties and had the wrinkled skin of a smoker. His hair was white, and it was cropped short. The top was as flat as a board.

Cove leaned on the inside of the doorway and faced the two. "Somebody find the body?"

Mendiola answered. "Yeah. It was clear down in Lemhi County."

"Any idea who he is?" Cove asked.

Mendiola and Erdos looked at each other. One of Mendiola's eyes squinted. After a moment, he turned back to Cove and shook his head. "You're thinking of Rodriguez's buddy. This one's got both feet. We're assuming it's Terzi."

Cove was jolted. He'd expected to hear this news a long time ago while he was in the hospital. But as the weeks–then months–went on, he'd started to doubt the body would be found. His brain had played tricks and had told him that somehow he'd survived and was still out there. There'd been times when he'd thought he'd heard footsteps, thought he'd smelled the man's acetone breath. He looked down at the file that Erdos had on his lap and felt the chipped molar with his tongue.

Mendiola spoke. "They pulled him out of the river just below the Pahsimeroi. He was in that straight stretch they call the glassy hole. It's possible it's not him, but it has to be."

"Who found him?" Cove asked.

"Some floaters." Mendiola said. "Thought it was a mannequin at first. They called it in here, but it was obvious it was across the county line. Didn't take Lemhi long for the recovery. I called Dave, and we went down and took a look after they had him bagged."

"Recognizable?" Cove asked.

"Face's mostly gone," Erdos said. "No hair. Smelled like rotten clams. Glad I didn't have to transport him. There's gonna be a fight over who pays for the goddamned autopsy. Technically it's theirs, but Williams says he's not gonna order one unless we pay for it. I'm gonna have to sit down with the commissioners."

"Who's Williams?" Cove asked.

"The coroner up there," Erdos explained.

"Can they pull prints?" Cove asked.

"Oh, no," Erdos said. "Way too late for that. It's gonna be dental or something else."

Mendiola turned to the coroner. "Tweekers aren't big on dentists."

Erdos found a thick multipage report in the folder and

held it up. "There's mention in here of recovering your knife at the scene and the theory that the blade broke off in his leg bone. Assuming it's him, that'll be a start but it's not gonna to be definitive. I'll need the knife."

Mendiola's eyes flashed to Cove momentarily. "It should still be in evidence."

"Charlie," Erdos said, "I've read over McGee's report and listened to your interview. It's an *odd story.*"

Cove's forehead wrinkled. The way he'd used the word "story" sounded as if it was short on the truth. "Odd story? What do you mean?"

"After I got out of the army, I spent twenty-six years with LAPD. We had lots of officer-involved shootings. We had several fatals from officers hittin' guys in the wrong places with their sticks. We used to carry the solid ash ones. This was before those goddamned side-handled ones come out. If you didn't want to call an ambulance, the only place you could lay into a schmuck was by hittin' him across his shins. I busted four sticks. They're hanging on my wall. We had officers that used their cruisers. But I never heard of a cop using a knife. Never. Nobody I've talked to had heard it either." Erdos stared at Cove for a second and looked back at the report.

Cove felt his ears begin to burn. "Dave?" He waited until Erdos looked up. "Were those batons the long black ones?"

"Yeah, had a leather loop on the handle so they wouldn't get away from you," Erdos answered.

"And the guys you busted them over," Cove's eyes drilled into the coroner's face. "What color were they?"

Erdos's eyes flickered. The muscles in his jaw

tightened. He closed the file, stood up and looked at Mendiola. "I gotta make some calls."

Cove watched the man walk out the door. It closed with a heavy thump. The female dispatcher at the far end of the room stared at her computer screen and acted as if there was no one else in the building.

"Jesus, Cove," Mendiola said. "You've got a way of slicing salami that'd piss off a fence post." He glanced at Cove's pant pocket. "Make sure I get the knife."

Cove raised his eyebrows and shrugged. "He started it... What'd his eyes look like?"

Mendiola's brow furrowed. "His eyes? The dead guy?"

Cove nodded. "Yeah."

"Williams unzipped the bag. I thought I was gonna blow. You know me, I can't handle the stink." Mendiola's skin blanched. "His face's 'bout gone. What's left of it looked like it was carved from a block of yellow soap." The crowfeet at the sides of Mendiola's eyes tightened. "As long as it's not a kid, I can deal with it, but that odor. Jesus." He shook his head. "Don't ever touch a drowning vic without gloves. You can't wash it off." He brought his fingers to his nose. "I didn't touch him, and I can still smell it."

Cove studied him for a moment and considered repeating the question but let it go.

Chapter 17

Cove called Bob Johnson. While he listened to the ringing, he thought about his day. It'd been a long one. He looked at the clock on his dash. It was nearly dinnertime.

Johnson answered, and Cove asked about the sample. "What do you mean, the lab says the water was clean? It can't be."

"The PH was 7.2, just where it should be. It had a little arsenic, but way below EPA levels. Probably better than the water out of your tap," Johnson explained.

Cove hesitated. He liked solving puzzles, but this one wasn't happening. He'd found that to solve a mystery, he had to come up with a theory on what had happened and how it had occurred. That theory would guide him to the evidence. If the evidence wasn't there, he'd modify the theory and keep working it out. This method had found the phone, and it had found the blood spatter. But without a theory to focus on for the West Fork, he found himself faltering. All that he found was unexplained death.

"Nothing else?" Cove asked.

"Arsenic and acidity. That's usually what mines put

out. That's what I had them test for. There's a gazillion tests they could run, but that's not the way they do things. When they called me up and gave me the results, I thought *what the hell* and told them to run it for mercury. They did. It came back clean for that too. I'm not sure what to tell you. If we come up with some other idea, we can send them another sample."

Cove told him about the lack of aquatic insects, algae and the dead doe. He suggested his field crew electroshock the stretch to see if it had been re-inhabited by any fish. It got the old biologist's attention.

"That's weird. I can't believe that doe has anything to do with this. That's got to be something else. My crew's working the Lemhi tribs this week. I can bring them up next week. We should at least shock Morgan Creek, and see how extensive this is."

After the call he thought about Duran. She was a breath of fresh air, attractive and intelligent. She'd offered to buy him a steak for dinner and it sounded like she'd be in town tonight. And he was hungry. He called Julie.

"They pulled a body out of the river today."

"Is it him?" she asked.

"They don't know yet. Sounds right. I'm tempted to run to Salmon and take a look." Cove thought about what the body must look like. The only thing he had to compare it with was a bighorn sheep that had been dumped off a bridge, and he'd found it months later in the river. It was headless with a bullet in its chest. The hair had come off, exposing its slick white skin, and the only way he could identify it as a sheep and not a deer was by its larger heart-shaped hooves. Cove was sure a viewing of this human's body was something he didn't want to add to the closet in his head.

Cove exhaled. "I can't believe there's enough left that I could ID him." There was a part of him that wanted to look at this dead body. Confirm that Leo Terzi was truly dead.

Cove and Julie talked for about five minutes. She told him about stories she was chasing and he updated her on the West Fork. They didn't talk about dreams. They didn't talk about whatever relationship was left between the two of them.

After he hung up, he called Spark's landline. "How's the headache?"

"Feels like somebody's beating a bass drum."

"How deep of shit am I in with George?"

"Deep enough to get him to send a text to you. I never thought I'd see that."

"Why'd he do that? What was that all about?"

"Your phone acted like it was in a dead spot. I told him to try a text message... that sometimes they'd get through when a call wouldn't. I guess it worked."

"What did he say after I went back into the sheriff's office?" Cove asked.

"He seemed to settle down after you told us what Wilson had given up. Said the word was going to be out that we were watching the Holman hole. He's kinda hard to read."

"Before you send your use-of-force report to him, let me take a look at it. Been there. And let me know when you've got a new cell phone."

Cove turned up Garden Creek and headed to his house. His phone buzzed. It was Duran. He studied the screen for a moment. After it vibrated again, he pressed the sleep button and put the phone back in his pocket.

He thought about the Cat's Ears, and the broken knife he'd left at the top. After the sage smudge, he'd slept until daylight and felt rested the next day. It had been a good night. The dream he had that night hadn't haunted him. He needed to go back. Spend another night. Study the circle. What he didn't want to do was remove his broken knife from the hill.

Erdos believed the knife was stored in evidence and available. Mendiola assumed Cove still had it and would hand it over. He might have to tell Mendiola a lie.

When he got home, he fed Annie and took the bottle of Jack Daniel's off the top of the refrigerator. He filled a glass tumbler with ice and poured whiskey into it. He wasn't going to the Cat's Ears. Not tonight.

***

The echoes of the gunshot woke him. The noises and chaos were as vivid as a 3D IMAX movie. At some point in the dream, his view had shifted from outside his body as if he were on the ceiling or in the sky. He'd seen his own red blood and pink brains spattered across the trailer's white wall and had watched Terzi disappear into the river. He'd never seen that in the dream before, it had always ended with his own death. And in this dream, like the others, there'd been no shadows.

He was awake and sweaty. The noise of the gunshot still rang in his ears. His heart was pounding, and his head hurt. He felt like he needed to go back to sleep, but he didn't want to live the dream again–feel the barrel in his mouth–hear Julie's screams and watch his own death.

He swallowed three aspirin and didn't bother to look at the clock. The steaming shower settled him down. He made a pot of hot coffee and bounced around on the Internet. He read the Char-Koosta news and caught up on the happenings on the rez. He read Julie's most recent articles and Googled Mexican cartels and trout diseases. Finally, he tried to find an image of what a drowning victim's eyes looked like after six months in the river. He wanted to see if they were as pale as opaque marbles.

After two hours he sent a text message to Mendiola, asking if he wanted to meet for breakfast.

***

At six-thirty, they had the place to themselves. The sun was still behind the Big Lost Range, but the night sky was gone. Traffic was picking up on the highway in front of the restaurant.

"I'm thinking about heading to Salmon and looking at the body."

"What in the hell for?" Mendiola asked.

Cove shrugged. "Help ID it. See if it's really him."

"You don't understand what the Goddamned river does. Besides, you've burnt that bridge."

Cove's eyes narrowed. "What do you mean, bridge?"

"It ain't in Salmon–or it's not gonna be. Erdos is taking it down to get it autopsied today." Mendiola's face frowned. "Sometimes you forget how small this town is. I remember telling you eight years ago that you'll catch more flies with honey. Dave's not the first asshole you've pissed off."

Cove was expecting Fred to ask for the broken knife. He poked a piece of bacon in his egg yolk, chewed on it and washed it down with coffee. The liquid tasted bitter and burnt. He spooned sugar into his mug.

"Allergies acting up?"

"No, why?" Cove asked.

"Eyes are red," Mendiola said with a frown.

The conversation lapsed, and the two worked on their food. The waitress filled their mugs. An old rancher came in, waved at the two officers and sat near the door.

"I didn't get a chance to tell you yesterday, but McGee's boss came up with a crew, and they went over Rodriguez's truck. Three ISPs and a blood spatter gal from the lab."

"And?"

Mendiola nodded. "She's cute. I shoulda introduced you."

"You're a perv."

"Just trying to find you a woman, Cove. I like challenges. Speaking of which, Duran was trying to find you last night. She looked hungry. Said she owed you dinner. I don't think that's what she was thinking about. Where the hell were you?"

"What'd they come up with?"

"You were right." Mendiola's black eyebrows came up. "She said it's consistent with blowback spatter."

"They swab it for DNA?"

"Yeah, she did. And I told McGee's boss about the shell casings you and Jenks recovered and asked him about the scene in Arizona. Told him that you said yours was from a

Glock. He lit up and was on the phone to Arizona for twenty minutes. Stared at McGee the whole fuckin' time." Mendiola glanced at the rancher and lowered his voice. "I looked at both casings. I should've had you take a peek. But I think they're the same." He nodded. "Arizona recovered three shell casings at the Talavera scene. Their lab says they were fired from a .45 Glock. The Poky lab's gonna send some pics down to Arizona. I got the idea the casings and the DNA's a priority... There's a reason I got ISP on this." Mendiola took a drink of coffee. "I'll give it two, maybe three days and Arizona'll have a warrant for Rodriguez. Somebody'll catch him doing twenty-five in a school zone—I don't care what shittin' state he's in—he's gonna get hooked and there ain't gonna be no fuckin' bail. Not an illegal with a history and grabbed for murder. And I'll betcha a hunter's gonna find a body this fall with one foot and even Pallid'll have to chase this thing to the end."

"Erdos going to leave the body in Pocatello?"

"Jesus Christ, Charlie. Leave it alone."

Cove rubbed his eyes and thought about all the nights he'd awoken at 3:43 and how Julie had reacted to the revelation. He looked at Mendiola. "You ever figure out what time Terzi snatched Julie?"

The sheriff's eyes squinted. "You're stuck in the past, Charlie. Stuck in a trailer on Ruby Creek." His tongue rubbed across the inside of his lip. He looked like he had a pinch of Skoal in his mouth. "No. We didn't. I'm guessing it was well after the bars closed. Before sunup. What difference does it make?" Mendiola glanced at the rancher and it looked like he was trying to listen. He leaned towards Cove and lowered his voice. "Charlie. Terzi's dead.

Julie's fine. I don't know what you're working on in Morgan Creek, but it can wait. It's fish for Christ's sake. Take some time off. Go to Boise. Try to make a baby. Don't let the damn job chew you up."

Cove's phone vibrated. He pulled it out of his pocket and looked at the screen. "It's your dispatch." He slid his finger across it and brought it to his ear.

"Charlie," a female voice said, "there's two people here who want to talk to you."

"Who are they?"

"They wouldn't say. And they asked for Officer Charles Cove. They're not from around here. They're dressed up."

Cove promised to be at the sheriff's office in a few minutes. He hung up and told Mendiola what he'd just heard.

"Charles." Mendiola was frowning. "It's like they got it off your driver's license... Almost sounds like the feds. They usually tell me when they're coming, though." He looked at Cove, his face deadpan. "If they're starting a civil rights investigation, I'd think they'd have called me, maybe not." He shook his head. "It'd be bullshit."

When Cove pulled in behind the courthouse, he could see a man and a woman sitting on the steps of the sheriff's office. They were both in their thirties and looked relaxed but attentive. Both were conspicuously well groomed. The man was wearing dark slacks, a white shirt and a herringbone sport coat and held a notebook in his hands. His hair was blond and neatly combed. She was slender and wore an olive-green pantsuit, matching jacket and a lacy white blouse. Her hair was long and black and her skin was maybe from the Middle East. They didn't look like cops. They looked more like attorneys.

When Cove opened his truck door, they stood up. She wore black spiked heels that exposed her toes and nails that were painted the same color as her outfit. He had on polished slip-on shoes that looked new and expensive. The two stuck out like a couple of Russian wolfhounds at the pound and had Cove's attention.

The woman spoke first. "Officer Charles Cove?"

He nodded. "I go by Charlie."

"I'm Raika Kashani." She handed him a business card. "This is Patrick Dayton."

Cove looked at the card. His brain hung for a moment. "Valley News? ...I think the sheriff will be here in a bit." He looked up. "You must have driven up last night?"

Cove assumed this was over the cartel and the foot. He wasn't going to talk about it, and he didn't understand why they hadn't asked for Mendiola.

"We left this morning. It's a hot story." Dayton said. "This is gorgeous country up here." The way he said it, made him sound like someone who wasn't coming back.

The woman turned to her partner. "Patrick, why don't you get the camera out of the car?"

"Time out," Cove said. They were focused on *him*. "What's this about?"

The man pulled a camera from the sliding door of a white van that was parked nearby.

The woman smiled with teeth that were too white and lips too full. "Just a sec, officer."

"No." Cove's face was like a rock. "You turn that camera on, and I drive off. Please, what's this about?"

"We understand they found Leonard Terzi's body."

Cove's ears started to hum and for a moment his jaw hung open. "It hasn't been identified yet."

Dayton handed her a mike. Cove glanced at him and warned, "I'm sorry, but there's not going to be an interview." A red light glowed on the camera.

"Officer."

Cove turned back to Kashani. She had the mike to her chin. "Could you tell us––"

"I'm sorry. It's not going to happen."

***

Cove was wound like a spindle. When he turned onto the highway, he could see the Cat's Ears, and it brought back the sweet smell of sage smoke. He relaxed a bit. He remembered that he'd felt as untroubled as the earth was old, but was also a bit mystified by what had happened that night. When he crossed over Ruby Creek, he thought of the river rocks he'd collected and dumped by his picnic table below his house. He knew what he needed to do. Life was talking to him, but he had a problem that was weighing him down. It'd have to wait.

He parked his truck in the cottonwoods along the West Fork. Stepping out, it felt good to be back in the hills. He'd decided to leave Annie at home. It had been a dilemma. He knew he could use her senses. Her nose and ears. But if the water was poisonous enough to kill a doe–and he didn't know that it was–he wasn't going to risk his dog. He crossed the West Fork on the same downed log. Picking up a rock in the creek, he confirmed there were still mayfly and caddis larvae above Fourth Spring Creek.

When he got near the doe, he could hear ravens talking. This time it wasn't one or two. It sounded like a dozen. It was what he expected. But when he saw the carcass, he was surprised. She was still intact. He believed she'd been dead for three days now. Three days is a long time in the woods for a dead doe. The only scavengers that had touched her were the ravens. They'd pecked on her eyes and mouth. The rest of the doe was untouched. During the day, the winds had blown up the drainage and at night they'd come back down. For three days and nights, this wind had pulsed back and forth. It should have attracted every bear, wolf, and coyote for five or more miles. But there'd only been a handful of ravens working it. Ravens were omnivores, and their long blunt beaks were handy for eating many foods–but they couldn't rip deer hide. There was a reason these birds were so raucous. They needed something with fangs to open up the deer's hide and share the meat that was inside. These birds had probably found this doe the day she died. They'd called for their brothers and sisters for days now, and no one had shown to carve up the feast. It was another sign that something wasn't right.

Cove continued up the drainage. For a hundred yards the odor of the doe's decomposition followed him. When the smell left him, he cut over to the creek and studied it for a moment.

He could have driven around the southwest side of Fourth Spring Creek, parked at the top, and dropped down. But he'd come up from the bottom in the belief that by checking the creek for insects, much like a prospector with a gold pan, he could discover the source of whatever was killing the creek without overlooking something.

The creek looked fine. The rocks on the bottom were a deep red-brown, and not the yellowish color that Johnson had told him to look for. It smelled rich, and the air was cool. Pulling a black nitrile glove from his pocket, he put it on, and picked up a fist-sized rock. It was dark red and angled. Its edges were acute and not rounded like the stones in the West Fork. There were no aquatic insects on the rock, and its surface felt like sandpaper. It looked like a rock that someone had picked off the hillside and dipped in the water. Not like it'd been in the creek for decades or longer. He set it back in the creek and studied the vegetation. Both sides of the creek were vibrant and green with tall grasses and thick clumps of willows. The leaves on these tall woody plants were long and the color of Chinese jade.

Moving up the slope, he found a twelve-foot tall lodgepole pine sapling that was missing most of its bark and limbs up to about the six foot level. A few yards up the hill, there was another sapling that was also beaten. He found a hair that was stuck in the dried pitch and brought it to his eyes. It was the long dark-brown hair from the mane of a bull elk. Cove judged the trees had been used for sparring partners the previous September and perhaps the year before by the same bull.

The drainage was beginning to dogleg to the right, its sides forming a steep V. The firs were getting bigger, and he'd passed a few large ponderosa pines. The forest floor was carpeted with a bed of dark red needles. He could see where the drainage benched out eighty-yards above him, and he assumed it was where the bull had found a flat spot to bed. Cutting up towards it, a sour skunky odor cut his path for a second, but the breeze turned and it was gone. It had been faint, and he hadn't recognized it. He stood still for a minute, listened and wished he could watch Annie's nose. He was far enough from the creek that he no longer heard its murmur. The breeze came up the hill and cut through the canopy above him like a ghost. The needles on the limbs rustled and stirred the hillside. Then it was gone, and the forest was quiet except for a two-noted "fee-bee" call from a chickadee farther up the mountain. It was the first bird he'd heard since the ravens.

He moved silently up, unable to see much farther because of the lip that formed above him. The taste of whatever had caught him had his hackles up. The hill below the bench became steeper. He found an old game trail that angled upwards, and he began following it. When he reached the edge of the bench, he froze like an icicle hanging from the edge of a cliff. It was set at shin level and he would have missed it if the sun hadn't lit it up.

Chapter 18

It had been stretched across the trail. His first reaction was that it was a thin cable–something that you'd hang a picture frame with. Without bending over, he followed it with his eyes to the right. It ended at a tree about ten yards away. Following the thread to the left, his eyes saw the same thing. He exhaled. It wasn't tied to a device. It wasn't a set-gun. There was no shotgun barrel pointing at his pelvis. It was gray thread.

He walked to the end of the thread and studied the knot. It appeared to be common sewing thread. It was too fine to determine the type of knot that had been used. He couldn't see any lichens or moss or bark that had blown on or grown into the thread. It looked as if it could have been tied between the trees the night before or last week or last month but certainly this summer.

In the winter, Cove kept a spool of white thread that he used to enforce the seventy-two hour rule for trap sets. By law, a trapper had to check his traps every seventy-two hours. The legislature had decided that if an animal–with its foot caught in a leg hold trap–remained any longer than three-days, it was suffering. If there wasn't snow on the ground, it was difficult to enforce. Cove had found that trappers had a tendency to use the same path to check each set. Just like any other demographic, some trappers followed the rules and some didn't. When they didn't, it caught Cove's attention since he believed that any animal in a leg-hold trap was suffering as soon as the steel jaws slammed shut. He had found that stretching a nearly invisible thread across the path would tell him how often a trap was being checked.

The only reason Cove could think that this thread had been placed was to determine if someone or some animal were using the trail. He stepped back to the edge of the bench and studied the hillside below him. He concluded that if anyone or any critter was going to climb to the bench, the terrain and vegetation would funnel them onto this trail. Looking towards the creek, he guessed he was about two hundred yards from it and about a mile up from the West Fork where he'd parked his truck. Thinking back to when he'd previewed Fourth Spring Creek using Google Earth, he estimated he was about halfway between the bottom of the drainage and the top. No matter which direction one came from to get to this place, it was a two-mile round-trip hike in steep country. He couldn't think of a legitimate reason for the thread. When he'd come up the trail, it'd been dusty and there weren't any footprints. He hadn't seen any human sign below him, and he decided that whomever had left the thread had probably driven up the Fourth Spring road and had come from above. There were lots of things he had expected to find in Fourth Spring Creek, but this wasn't one them.

Cove looked at the trail beyond the thread. There were no tracks. Looking behind him, the outline of his boot prints in the dust stuck out like stencils. He dropped back off the hill, walked to the creek and cut a heavily leafed willow limb with his pocketknife. He picked up a rock from the creek's bed and checked it for insects. It was clean. Working back up the trail, he brushed away his tracks with the willow leaves. It left a few scratch-like marks, and it didn't look perfect, but it didn't look like someone had come up the trail.

Cove walked around the thread and looked at the bench. The vegetation was thicker, and it limited the distance he could see. It was fairly flat but still had a slight slope up towards the head of the drainage. He recalled what it looked like on his computer. It was a long banana-shaped step that curved along the hillside, perhaps a hundred yards wide. He'd thought it looked like a good place to find an elk–lush and green. Tall grasses covered the forest floor. The trees had transitioned to quaking aspens, intermixed with a few ponderosa pines. The chickadee that he had heard from below the bench repeated its call from the aspen farther up, and he felt his breathing settle down.

He walked beside the trail. The only track he saw in the dust belonged to a tree squirrel that had angled over to a pine. About sixty yards from the thread, he found a black pan sitting in the grass. The pan was heavy rubber. It had an inch or so of a thick-green liquid in it and two dark lumps that looked like dead mice. Cove dropped to one knee, cupped his hand and brought the air above the liquid to his nose. He caught the candied smell of antifreeze. The wrinkles on his forehead tightened.

Cove looked farther along the bench and felt the stubble on his cheeks. This pan made less sense than the thread. But together, it could only mean that somebody wanted to poison wildlife, and the thread was to monitor trail activity. He had no idea if the thread was to detect humans or animals or both, but either way, why? And why the poison?

He turned the pan over and dumped the antifreeze out. The breeze shifted, rustling the aspen leaves and it brought the skunky odor back to his nose. It almost smelled like dirty socks in a gym bag or a food cache made by a pack rat, but he knew it wasn't a rodent's pantry. And it sure as hell wasn't a skunk. His hackles came up. It was stronger now, and whatever it was didn't belong in the Salmon River country. Something was seriously out of his box.

He moved forward as if he were hunting. He'd take three soundless steps and then stop. At each pause, he'd study the breaks in the vegetation ahead of him and listen. Other than the whisper of the aspen leaves, it was quiet. Before he'd start moving again, he'd glance at the ground and ensure his feet weren't going to disturb a stick or a rock. He'd make a quick check behind him, and then take three more slow steps.

After several more yards, Cove spotted a fat black line laying in the grass and angling off to his right. It was about an inch in diameter and was polyethylene pipe. For a moment, his brain stuttered. He knelt down and put his fingers on it. It was cold. He finally had a theory.

He eased up and began following the pipe back

towards the north, somewhat in the direction of his truck. Within sixty yards, he caught an emerald green that he hadn't seen on the bench. It was much more vibrant than the leaves of the aspen and lighter than the fir needles. Within a few more yards, he was sure of what he was looking at. The plant was about four-feet tall and its long serrated leaves looked like thin fingers radiating from a palmless hand. Cove eased over to it and noticed that a piece of 1/4" tubing had branched off the pipe and fed this plant through a drip nozzle that was producing several drops of water per minute. A pungent oily odor hovered around the plant.

Looking down the bench, he could see several other plants. He walked over, counted ten more and confirmed the main pipe stopped. None of the plants had been foraged on.

Cove pulled his phone out and checked for service. There were no dots showing any signal. He opened his text program, selected Mendiola and typed; "Possible grow in Fourth Spring Creek." He pressed send but didn't feel optimistic. While the phone was attempting to find a tower, he looked up the drainage, studying the bench. There was still no bird activity and nothing moved. His phone vibrated once. "Message Failed to Send."

Cove had two choices. Back out and return with help or continue up the drainage and figure out whether this site had a dozen or so plants—or hundreds. He was aware of marijuana grows that had been discovered on the west side of the state that had thousands of plants. If this was a small grow, whoever was running it was probably commuting. If it was large, he assumed they'd be camped somewhere above him.

The antifreeze made sense. Deer were known to eat marijuana, and they were known to drink antifreeze. It'd kill them. He assumed that bears and coyotes and anything else would drink it and die. It explained why no four-legged critter had fed on the doe. However, he didn't know the mechanism of death or how far a poisoned animal would travel after drinking it, but he didn't think the doe would have made it a half-mile down the hill. But what else could have killed her? Had he missed another pan full of the poison? He believed the shin-high thread was a symptom of the dope grower's paranoia about being discovered.

A mile below, locked in his truck, he had an AR-15 rifle and a portable radio. He wished he'd brought both of them. He assumed that anyone cultivating marijuana would be armed. He felt comfortable with his Glock, but a pistol was only good to about twenty-five or thirty yards in a gunfight. It'd be no match for an AK-47 or some other rifle in the timber.

Cove moved back up along the pipe. His plan was to gather more information and back out undetected. Within a hundred yards, Cove found another pan of antifreeze. It had three dead mice in it. He thought about dumping the poison. One could blame the other empty pan on a bear, but if the grower found two empty pans, he'd probably come to one conclusion. He didn't like it, but he left the antifreeze in the pan and continued following the pipe. After thirty yards he located a T-junction with another piece of one-inch pipe heading off to the left. He found ten more plants along the edge of the bench next to the steep hillside. They were all spaced about fifteen feet apart and were beginning to bud.

He turned back and once again initiated his slow-motion walk along the pipe. It was angling towards the creek. When he got to the edge of the bench, the pipe contoured towards the creek. He found a game trail coming up to the bench and located another gray thread stretched across it. Above him, the creek was making much more noise than it had down by the doe. He dropped off the bench, followed the pipe and found a makeshift dam. It was made using two stacked logs that had been set across the channel. A piece of black plastic sheeting had been rolled across the top of the log. Water was pouring over it, making a racket. When he crawled above the dam, he could see that the plastic was also coving the bottom of the pool and was held down by rocks. The plastic pipe had been fished through the dam and was lying in the water. Set beside the pool were two black bulging garbage sacks. A plastic cup sat between them. Cove opened the first one. It contained a half-full vinyl bag of garden fertilizer. When he opened the other bag, a harsh garlic-chemical odor hit him. It had a heavy yellowish-brown paper bag in it that was open. It was full of what looked like black poppy seeds. He peeled the garbage bag away and looked at the label. There were two skull and crossbones printed on the sticker. In between were bold capital red letters: "POISON." The other word that jumped at him from the label was "Temik." He held his breath and pulled the plastic bag back up.

The noise from the creek spilling over the logs was so loud that someone could come up behind him and tap his shoulder with a gun barrel. He moved up the hill and got back on the bench and far enough away from the creek to where he could listen. He stopped at a ponderosa tree and thought about what he'd just found. He'd sat in on a briefing about Temik. The stuff was deadly. Temik was so toxic that if someone were to handle it without gloves and a respirator, they'd expect to go into convulsions in a matter of minutes. The EPA had recently banned its use in the United States. It had been illegally used as a wolf poison in Idaho and Wyoming. It was a Bayer product, and it had been legally used in the production of beans and peanuts and many other food crops for many years. In Idaho it had been used on potatoes and had taken over DDT's niche. If one followed the instructions for Temik, it was tilled into the ground at planting time with the seed potato or whatever it was protecting. As the plant grew, it took up the poison in its roots and then its leaves. Insects that ate the leaves or roots died. The problem was that if *anything* ate the plant, it died. And if the crop was harvested before 90 days, the food was poisonous to humans. It'd been banned because it remained poisonous to kids well after the time it hit the supermarkets. Cove realized that if this marijuana grower were still adding Temik to his irrigation system, then the dope would be poisonous.

Cove put a hand on the red bark of the ponderosa and felt its rough surface. The pesticide in the creek explained the dead doe and the havoc in the West Fork. Between the Temik and the antifreeze, it clarified why the only birds he'd heard in Fourth Spring Creek were the ravens and one chickadee. Listening to the hillside, it was still quiet.

Not a bird.

Cove had accompanied his father hunting when he was too small to carry a rifle. They'd sit with their backs to a tree and listen to the woods. Unequivocally, the sounds that stood out were the bird calls. They almost always made noise. If things got quiet or their tenor changed, his father would point it out. Cove recalled one such morning when his father had gestured towards a grove of trees where a flute-like chirping was coming from and said, "That's a robin. He's thinking about catching some food for his kids. He's happy." His father had instructed Charlie to sneak up on the bird and try to locate it before it saw him. His father had explained, "When it sees you, it'll say 'peek-peek-peek' and then fly off." He hadn't seen the robin, but he'd heard the alarm call.

The bench sounded hollow without birds. Cove felt blind. The trees limited his vision to less than sixty yards; in some places, much less. His eyes were no better than anybody else's. And if there was a person working this grow, Cove had a fifty-fifty chance of seeing him first. He was partially deaf in his left ear, but somehow his brain had compensated, and he was usually able to tell from what direction a noise came from—if he heard it.

He checked his phone. No service. He'd found twenty-one marijuana plants. By any standard, this was a small grow. Cove thought about this fact. He knew that it was still worth a significant amount of money. He recalled being stunned at the police academy to hear that a pound of high-grade marijuana went for as much as three-thousand dollars on the streets of Boise, and that one plant could produce a pound of pot. To a small-time pothead in Challis, twenty-one plants represented a considerable chunk of change. Whoever was running this grow had to be checking to make sure the irrigation pipe wasn't plugged, was probably throwing a few cups of fertilizer into the pool at each visit, perhaps stupid enough to continue adding the Temik.

Cove's ancestors had marked a year by its thirteen moons and four seasons. Other times of the year were marked by annual cycles like the blooming of the bitterroot, the spawning of cutthroat or the thunder-like crash of a bighorn ram striking an opponent's horns. They had names for the different phases of the moon, and in essence, they were their weeks. He didn't think they had names for the days; no Mondays or Sundays. But that was then and this was now. Cove believed that whoever was cultivating these plants wasn't doing it by the phase of the moon. He was dancing to a different drum than the Salish would have done generations ago. He was probably doing it once a week. Once every seven days. If he had a job– besides growing dope–he was probably climbing down to this garden on a day off. Probably each Saturday. Three days from today. Assuming this wasn't somebody's full-time job and he–or they–were camped somewhere in the drainage.

The breeze shifted, and the odor of marijuana briefly touched his nose. He looked at the shimmering aspen leaves and decided it could have come from farther up the canyon. After another fifty yards, he noticed a pole that was at an odd upright angle with something hanging from it. It consisted of a dry lodgepole sapling attached to two trees with heavy wire. The pole's tip was a dozen feet off the ground. A piece of nylon cord had been tied to it and hung down to the level of Cove's throat. At its end, there was a large three-pronged fishhook baited with dried meat. It smelled like venison. The bait had been on the hook at least a week, maybe much longer. The treble hook had been tied with a double overhand knot. He untied it and tried to remove the bait, but the meat was hard and clung to the barbs on each of the hooks. He finally got the bait off with his knife. He pushed the bare hook into the ground with his boot. There was no way he was going to leave this device hanging. If a coyote or wolf or bear had found it, it would have died a horrible death. Cove understood why the grower was using the antifreeze to poison deer. And the same went for using the pesticide to protect the crop from insects. But this, hanging this baited treble hook, he didn't understand. It made no sense other than whoever had hung it was an evil bastard.

Chapter 19

Cove looked back at the nylon cord hanging from the pole. It was twisted where the knot had been and looked like a pigtail. If it was discovered by the growers, it could be interpreted that a bear or some other animal had been hooked and the knot had come undone. So he was okay with leaving one more signature that he'd been here.

He really wanted to find this bastard, but he was a realist. Taking down a grow wasn't like pinching someone for fishing without a license. Even if he could find a spot with cell service, it'd take backup an hour to get to Fourth Spring Creek and another hour or so to find him in the timber. After two hours, backup wasn't backup. He had one set of handcuffs on his belt and two sets in his truck over a mile away. If he got the drop on the bastard, he could cuff him and get him off the hill. But not if there were two or three bastards. Things would go to shit.

The bench was getting steeper. It was still flat, but it was beginning to get a slight uphill pitch to it. He continued his silent three-stepped movement, followed by a long pause. The length of the pause was dictated by the wind currents, how open the vegetation was, and what he heard, smelled or eyed; some small shape or color or perhaps a hanging broken limb, or a line of grass that leaned in at an unnatural angle.

By now, he really wished he'd brought Annie. Cove's right hand reached below his holster and felt where her head should have been. Her nose and hearing were well beyond anything that a human could duplicate, or for that matter even understand. He'd seen her sense a human several minutes before he had heard or seen the person. He'd watched her do this when the breeze was in her face, but also when the wind was at her back. Many times he'd seen her pull a scent from where a person had walked and react as if it were something much more than just a few molecules that didn't belong. He had a belief that she could smell fear–or perhaps even guilt or lawlessness. Something like a pheromone–especially when they didn't want to be found. It was something that science didn't understand. He believed that when he was on the hunt, she had an understanding when it was time for business. She loved people but also clearly grasped that sometimes the people he was looking for were not the kind she should nuzzle.

Working around clumps of aspen and deadfalls, it took Cove about fifteen minutes to move another hundred yards. Stopping, he studied a break between two aspen branches that didn't look right and caught a thin wedge of the emerald green of another marijuana plant some sixty yards off to the right. He eased towards it. When he worked around the aspen clump, sixteen marijuana plants came into view. When he got to them, he found another irrigation system consisting of quarter inch tubes. He followed them up a few yards to where they branched off from another piece of one-inch poly pipe, and it snaked back to the left towards the creek. He assumed that it'd lead to another makeshift dam and bags of fertilizer and pesticide.

Cove eased to the trunk of a ponderosa pine, pulled out his phone out and dropped to one knee. He could see a line of bent grasses where someone else had walked past the tree to the plants. He studied where he had just walked and confirmed he hadn't left a trail. Either someone wasn't walking as carefully as he'd been, or they'd been walking the same path over and over. The grass was still a vibrant green. If it had been days since the person had passed, he believed the plants should have recovered by now. But even so, with the thirty-seven plants he'd discovered, it was time to get off the hill. Looking at the top of the phone's face, there were still no service dots. He tapped into his text app and sent out a short message to Mendiola, in hopes that the phone would find a weak signal on the hillside. While he waited for the phone to indicate the message's status, he pondered his egress plan. He decided that he would move to the uphill side of the bench, hit the steep hillside and disappear into the dog hair timber, using a circuitous route down to his truck. The phone vibrated. Glancing at it, he saw what he'd assumed.

The explosion of a grouse busting into the air caused Cove's lungs to freeze. He hadn't seen it but guessed that it had flushed a hundred or more yards up the bench. It was probably a ruffed or dusky grouse, but either way, it didn't sound like the bird had chosen to pop into a tree for a mid-day siesta, and it was far too early to be choosing a roost tree for the night. It'd sounded like it had blasted out of fear. He studied his options and regretted not high-tailing it to the thick timber after he'd spotted the sixteen plants. There were enough aspens between him and the edge of the bench that if someone were coming, they'd pass and he could remain hidden. If there were growers walking down the edge of the bench, he should be able to remain unseen.

The trunk of the ponderosa that Cove was kneeling behind was about two feet thick and provided decent cover. He eased his head to the right side of the tree and looked in the direction where the sound had come. His vision was limited to somewhere between fifty and seventy yards by fir, pine and aspen. A wisp of air caused the aspen leaves to quiver, and he thought he caught the weighty alkaline smell of black ash from an old campfire. He decided he'd watch for five minutes and if nothing moved, he'd start his egress. The watching lasted for perhaps a minute before Cove saw something move through a tiny window in the vegetation. It had been a small flick of white that he'd caught off to the side of his stare. Just brief enough to wonder if he'd seen it. It could have been a deer's rump. Staring, he took a slow deep breath and caught it again, but this time he saw blue and white. It was a plaid shirt, and whoever was wearing it was walking towards him.

Cove moved his head back behind the tree as slow as a bug crawling across a rock. He drew his gun, stood up and turned himself perpendicular to the trunk to give himself better cover. If things were going to go to shit, he wanted to be able to move. He was focused on sound, but the pounding of the blood in his heart started to betray him.

His Glock was flat against his abdomen, held by his right hand. His finger rested along the frame above the trigger. He was tempted to slowly roll out, size up the threat, see how many there were and how they were armed. But for the moment he held the element of surprise and remained hidden. There was still hope that the growers were headed off to the left and they'd pass on by. Again, he wished he'd brought Annie, since he believed she would have set the alarm with a low growl, and they would have boogied several minutes ago.

He held the pose for what seemed like an hour, but it couldn't have been longer than a minute before he heard the first footsteps. He couldn't tell how many people were approaching, but it sounded as if they were headed towards the sixteen plants behind him. The steps were coming at what sounded like an unhurried pace but were approaching the tree.

It had to happen now. Cove popped out from the tree, brought the Glock up and focused his vision on the front site that was now pasted in the middle of the man's chest. "Don't move," boomed from Cove's lungs. The man froze ten yards away. Cove was on autopilot, his training at full throttle. Although his focus was on the front site of his weapon, his brain seemed to be looking through the man—not at him—and it enabled him an almost out-of-body view of the situation. One man. Frozen. Palms low and open. No visible weapon.

"Hands on top of your head." When the man complied, Cove shifted his focal plane from his front site to his opponent's face. His gut twisted. It was Armando Barreras.

"Goddamn it Barreras, get on your knees."

The Latino complied.

"Ease down to the ground. Flat. On your gut." There was no vibration in Cove's angry voice. It was short, abrupt and deep. It was commanding. The consequence of noncompliance was clear.

When Barreras was proned out, Cove had him move his arms straight out, roll his palms up and look away.

Cove studied the forest where Barreras had come from. Nothing moved. He holstered his Glock and grabbed the man's outstretched arm, locked his wrist in a gooseneck and planted both knees in the man's back with his arm locked upright between his legs. He had control.

Cove reached back with his left arm, and pulled his handcuffs from his belt pouch and lowered his voice to a deep whisper. "Goddamn it Armando, who all's up here with you?" Cove snapped a cuff onto the wrist and curled the arm tightly into the small of the man's back. "Give me the other arm."

Barreras complied, and Cove completed the handcuffing. Rolling Barreras over, he felt the outside of his pockets and located a folding knife, removed it and felt up and down his jeans. "Don't bullshit me. How many people?" Cove's face was as tight as a glass bottle.

"Just me."

Cove rolled him up on his butt. "One more time, Armando. Who all's here?" Cove watched his brown eyes.

"Nobody."

The man didn't blink. Didn't look away. But his arms were locked behind him, and Cove wasn't able to watch his hands respond to the question. He watched the dark eyes flitting a bit left and right.

"What are you thinking about, Armando?"

"How much trouble I'm in."

Cove recognized that the man hadn't paused. He hadn't had to think about his answer. Looking back up the drainage, Cove thought about what he had. Barreras was in an illegal patch of marijuana, or at least walking towards sixteen plants. He hadn't seen him do anything that proved his involvement. Armando's mention of being in trouble was an admission, but it had been said without being Mirandized. And without a statement or physical evidence, nothing was going to stick. Not the growing of marijuana, the hook set for whatever might grab it, the antifreeze in the pans, or the Temik in the creek that had devastated the West Fork.

Cove's face was stiff. His lips were tight and his eyes were pinched down. His brain had been flushed with adrenalin and then jolted by anger that had been salted with exasperation. He looked at Barreras and gave him his Miranda rights.

"Tell your story and no bullshit. You get one chance. No lies."

Barreras exhaled. "I have no choice. He was going to take my wife, my oldest." His eyes widened.

"Who you talking about?" Cove asked.

"The man from the hospital." Barreras's volume had risen in pitch. "Said his name is Juan. Said Marcos Ayala is dead. Am I going to prison?"

Cove looked back up the hill. "Keep your goddamned voice down... Where's he at?"

"I don't know. Me hizo desenterrar a alguien y le cortó

su pie."

"English, Armando."

"He had me dig up a body and cut off his foot."

Cove's eyes got tighter. "When was this?"

"Two days ago. He took it with him and left."

Cove's brain wasn't getting this. "You dug up a body and cut a foot off it?"

"He made me. I swear, señor, I didn't want to do it."

"Who'd you dig up? Who's body?"

Barreras shook his head. "I don't know. Mexican kid. Maybe eighteen. Marcos or Juan or whatever his name is said his boss had made a big mistake, and he left with the foot."

"Mistake?"

Barreras nodded toward the plants. "Planting this marijuana here. He said this is Sinaloa ground, and they weren't paying their cut."

"You see any bullet wounds?"

"They'll kill me and take my family to Mexico. Make my wife a whore."

Cove bit his lip. "Unless there's somebody on this hill you haven't told me about, I'm the only friend you've got." He paused and glanced back up the hill. "Armando, you need to spill your guts."

Barreras's shoulders sagged. "I didn't want to do this. I just wanted to work the hay harvest for Bob Harris."

"I found five hanging hooks baited with meat. Why'd you put 'em out?"

"I only know of two. They were here when he brought me." He looked down the hill. "One down below and the one by camp."

Cove's head turned. "What are they for?"

Barreras shook his head. "I think he's scared of bears."

"When's he coming back?"

"I don't know. He said he'd bring more food."

"Where'd he take the foot?" Cove asked.

"Dunno."

"Your truck up above?"

"No, I would have left and taken my family to North Dakota."

Cove hesitated. "What are you supposed to do here?"

"Keep the water running. Make sure nothing's eating the plants."

"How many plants?"

Barreras shrugged. "Dunno. Several hundred."

Cove's mouth watered. "The pesticide, the Temik. What'd he tell you about that stuff?"

"He told me to throw a cup in the water every few days."

"Why didn't you just walk away, go home? It'd take a day."

"He put a pillow case over my head." Armando met Cove's eyes. "Where we at?"

Cove took a deep breath and glanced up the hill. "Where's the body?"

"Near camp. I covered him back up and gave him a prayer. Made a cross."

"How many irrigation dams?"

"Bout a dozen."

"Temik at each one?"

Barreras shook his head. "There's another bag up above."

Cove took his cell phone out of his shirt pocket, hoping to see that it had service. "This place is going to be swarming with cops in a while."

Barreras stared into Cove's eyes for a moment and then shook his head. "Señor, my phone's in camp. I tried to call you. There's no service here."

For a moment, they studied each other's eyes. Finally Cove said, "Show me."

***

The camp was tucked next to the creek in a thick jungle of fir trees. An open lean-to tent had been constructed from a silver plastic tarp that had been secured over a horizontal pole. The pole had been lashed to trees with baling twine. A military surplus camouflage netting was thrown over the tarp. A blue nylon sleeping bag was spread out at the mouth of the shelter.

"Where's your phone?" Cove asked.

Barreras nodded towards the sleeping bag. "In my coat pocket."

The jacket was rolled up at the head of the bag and had been used as a pillow. Cove located it in a pocket. It was a cheap flip phone.

"It's turned off." Barreras said.

Cove pushed the green button and watched it boot up. When it was on, he toggled around and found the recent phone log and located his number. It was the only call in red. He interpreted that the color indicated that it had not been able to complete the connection.

Cove rubbed his ear and reached into his pant pocket.

"Let's get the cuffs off."

While Armando rubbed his wrists, Cove looked around the camp. There was a large log that had been cut and placed next to the fire ring. A blackened coffee pot sat next to the ashes. The fire was out and looked like it had been that way for some time.

"What have you got for food?"

Barreras pointed to a nearby horizontal pole that was lashed to two trees and was about ten feet off the ground. It made Cove think that somebody was planning on hanging elk or deer quarters from it. A burlap bag hung from it.

Armando said, "I got two cans of refried beans and a few tortillas left. There's some coffee, but I can't find any matches."

Cove looked at a stack of firewood next to the ashes. "Is there a saw around here?"

"It's up by the grave."

***

The grave was a low mound of dirt about two feet wide and six or seven feet long. There was a cross made from two sticks and tied together with baling twine at one end.

"How deep?"

"Maybe three."

"The other foot's gone too, isn't it?"

Barreras's head came up, and his eyes narrowed. "Si, señor... He covered it with pine needles after I put him back in the ground. I cleaned them off. Built the cross."

There was a small chartreuse chainsaw laying next to a

tree. It looked like something a weekend camper might buy at Walmart. Cove leaned over and examined the teeth on the chain. It was crusted with dried flesh.

"What the hell's he doing with the foot you cut off?"

Armando shook his head. "He called it a mensaje. A message."

The two walked back to the camp. Cove sat down on the log next to the fire and looked where the flames had been. He rested his forearms on his knees, rubbed his whiskers and thought about Armando, his wife and kids and how they just wanted to be happy. He thought about the footless young Mexican in the grave. He apparently had been killed by Rodriguez for the sole reason so that a foot could be cut off to send some macabre message.

After a few minutes, Cove spoke. "This's one hell of a mess, but I think it'll work out." He glanced at Armando. "In the legal word, you've got what they call a necessity defense. You didn't have a choice. I can see that. The U.S. Attorney's office will see it too. You did it under duress. I know somebody that can put you and your family in witness protection. They'll move you somewhere safe, but you'll have to testify against this bastard. He needs to go away." Cove massaged his thigh and felt the knotted scar tissue. "I can't tell you much more 'cause I've never done this witness protection thing, but you can trust the lady who'll make it happen... her name's Duran. She's a friend of mine. You and your family'll be safe."

Cove looked into the fire pit and let out a deep breath. He felt a natural urge to put his palms out and feel the warmth where the flames had been. He felt relieved. A breeze hit the tree canopy above him and caused a rustling noise. He looked up the drainage and caught movement sixty yards back in the trees. It was a man with his arm around a boy. He started to draw his weapon, but he heard a swooshing sound and turned towards Barreras in time to see a piece of firewood rushing towards his face. And then he was gone.

Chapter 20

The pain felt like two fires, one in each shoulder. His ears had a deep thrumming in them that sounded like an idling truck. At first Cove thought he was in a thick fog but then decided his eyes wouldn't focus. When the blur began to burn off, he watched a drop of blood falling in slow motion from his nose. It was round and shiny and took minutes to fall. Finally, it splattered into a coagulated puddle that lay on a bed of pine needles in front his boots. It didn't make sense. He assumed this was another dream until he watched a shadow move like shade from a thunderstorm over the blood puddle.

The slap brought him to his senses. The coppery taste of blood filled his mouth. He felt the handcuffs biting into his wrists, and he understood that his arms werc cuffed behind him and were roped to a pole or a limb above him. His feet were just touching the ground. He lifted his head up and tried to focus on the face in front of him.

"Bueno. I was getting tired of slapping you." It wasn't Barreras's voice.

The man slapped Cove again and for a few moments, the fog returned. When his vision cleared, he watched another drop of blood fall from his nose. It fell as slowly as the first one and finally hit the puddle. He noticed a spot of dried blood on the top of his boot. It looked like the drop on the boot from the crash, but it was round.

He realized this must be Rodriguez and he looked up again. The man was barrel chested and light skinned for a Mexican and had black curly hair. The hollows of his eyes were still bruised from the wreck. He wore dark pants and an untucked sport shirt. Cove recalled that there had been a kid with him. Looking past the man, he saw a child, maybe ten, sitting on the log by the fire pit twenty yards away. The kid was looking down, and his face was wet with tears. Cove looked around for Armando and back at the kid. He was Latino, and it dawned on Cove who he must be. The realization brought back the memory of Barreras blindsiding him with the club. *Why?*

Rodriguez glanced at the boy. "Meet Tomás, he's mi amigo."

Cove looked back at the man's dark eyes. His voice was a harsh whisper. "Where's his father?"

Rodriguez laughed and sucked on his cigarette. "He's down getting your truck. Tomás and I found it before we drove up here. We're gonna go for a ride. Get away from my garden. I have good recipe." He took another drag on his cigarette and blew it into Cove's face. "I call it gringo asado. Your GMC will make good oven." He looked back at the kid. "Tomás says he'll come back with it. I think he's right. What do you think?"

"How old was he?" Cove whispered and lowered his head.

Rodriguez gave him a puzzled look. "Who?"

The pain was needy. It was difficult to stay focused.

"The kid that's buried up above."

Rodriguez inhaled his cigarette, his eyes became narrow and stared at him.

"The kid you killed." His voice was becoming more ragged. Cove brought his head back up and looked at the man. "He was sitting in your truck and you shot him." He felt his arms stretching, his joints coming apart. "You're chickenshit."

Rodriguez dropped the cigarette in the duff and punched Cove in his gut, knocking the wind from his lungs. He collapsed and leaned into his shoulder sockets. The pain put him deeper into the mist.

He felt himself drifting like a tumbleweed in an August wind. After a while, the fog thinned, and he realized it was sage smoke. He was back on top of the Cat's Ears. He couldn't move his arms. Somebody else was beating the raven's wing, washing him with the sweet smoke. It flowed around his chest and into his mouth. He looked at the fingers holding the wing. They were dark and thick. The person's other hand held the sage stick. The light was behind the man and came from the full moon that glowed white in the black sky. The man's face was dark, hidden by his own shadow. He brought the sage to his lips and blew on the fire. The embers flared and illuminated his father's face. His father's voice sounded like a flute, and Cove realized he was speaking Salish. Somehow he understood the words. The sound wasn't coming through his ears; it was as if the words were in him. His father held the burning sage and moved the smoke around Charlie with the wing and continued talking in Salish.

A younger voice cut through the smoke. He opened his

eyes and for a moment he didn't know where he was. His vision was fuzzy, but he could see Tomás yelling. The pain in Cove's shoulders had disappeared and had been replaced by a dense numbness. He could no longer feel his arms, and his head felt as heavy as a rock.

Rodriguez was laughing at Tomás. The kid had a knife in his hand and was pointing it at Rodriguez. The little kid's face was flushed and he yelled. "Let him go! Let him go!"

"You want to cut somebody?" Rodriguez asked. "Slice the gringo, mi amigo." He motioned towards Cove. "Gringos like it when you cut their face."

"I'm Salish." It was less than a whisper.

Rodriguez wheeled and looked at him with a tight-lipped smile. "I thought you were gone and wouldn't feel the fire. I was——" His eyes snapped wide and his mouth sagged.

Cove heard a loud crack. It echoed off the hillside. Rodriguez looked down at his chest. He was wearing a yellow short-sleeved shirt and a dark stain was forming under his armpit. Blood was running down his arm. He turned and brought his hand up and watched a drop form on his wrist. Another loud crack re-echoed from the timber. Rodriguez fell on his face.

Cove closed his eyes and leaned into the rope. He wasn't sure what he'd just seen or even *if* he'd seen it. He was tired and didn't trust his mind anymore. And he wasn't sure what his father had said.

After a moment in the fog, Cove could hear sobbing. He raised his head and saw Armando Barreras hugging his son. He was holding an AR-15 behind the kid's back.

Armando looked at Cove. "Señor, I'm sorry I busted your nose. If you'd pulled your gun, I knew what he'd do to Tomás. I had to do something." He walked over and cut the rope that was holding Cove up. Cove dropped to the ground with a groan. His arms began to tingle.

Barreras pulled Cove's key ring from his pocket and unlocked the handcuffs.

Epilogue

Cove added wood to the fire. He pulled a dome tent out of a nylon stuff sack and assembled the six fiberglass poles. Annie sat next to the creek and watched with her head on her paws. He slipped a pole through the tent's sleeve and secured its ends through grommets that protruded from webbing near the floor. A kingfisher chattered from around the creek's bend. He looked at his watch. It was nearly nine, and the sky was turning the magical dark-steel color in between day or night. He took off his watch and set it on the picnic table next to the bottle of Jack Daniel's, stripped down to his nylon shorts and felt the smooth pebbles on the beach with the soles of his feet.

The creek bank had been flushed clean by snow run-off and had left a flat bar that consisted of pea gravel and fine sands. Tall cottonwood trees lined the banks. The bark was dark gray and had convoluted ridges. On the north sides of the trunks, there were splotches of orange lichens. The heavy dark green leaves on the trees formed a broken canopy above him.

This place was just below Cove's house and owned by his neighbor, who used the nearby pasture to feed his cows in the winter. He'd let Charlie put in a fire pit and the wooden picnic table and use it whenever he wanted.

Cove finished putting up the tent and threw three old blankets over the top. Unzipping the door, he slid inside and cut a quarter of the floor out with his knife.

He stepped back to the table and sat down on its top. Picking up the bottle, he read its black label in the firelight. Jack Daniel's Tennessee Whiskey, 80 proof. He opened it up. The vapors struck his nose and his gut flinched. It smelled a bit like old burnt wood. He stood up and poured the whiskey into the edge of the popping fire. It hissed, and a cloud of steam rose up, disappearing into the darkening sky.

Cove dipped a coffee can into the creek and filled it. He set it inside the tent. Picking up a shovel, he scooped a cantaloupe sized river rock out of the fire. It had been there for over an hour and was almost glowing. He set it inside the tent where he'd removed the floor. He placed two more rocks beside it.

Cove entered the tent, pulled the blankets over the door, zipped it shut and sat down. He could feel the warmth coming from the rocks. He stuck his hand inside the coffee can and palmed water onto the stones. Steam hissed up and his body was hit by the sudden heat. He lowered his chin to his chest and felt the sweat running from his pores. Salt stung his eyes. He closed his mouth and breathed through his nose.

His tongue found the sharp edge on his broken molar,

and he thought about Leo Terzi. He had been ID'd by comparing his tattoos and old booking photos. His body was never claimed and was cremated by the county. He had no idea what they'd done with the box of ashes. The death certificate had been signed by the coroner and Cove had never bothered to hear what the official manner of death was. He no longer cared. Terzi was dead. Both Terzi and the dreams were in the past. He didn't call it closure. It was a memory.

He thought about Rodriguez. For an unexplained reason, the Mexican consulate in Salt Lake had come for the body. Again, he didn't care. His death certificate gave the manner of death as *legal homicide by a police officer*. Fred Mendiola had cooked up the idea to protect Armando Barreras and had somehow twisted Dave Erdos's arm hard enough to sign the document.

His brain shifted over to the footless body. The pathologist had estimated that the kid was a Latino between eighteen and twenty-one years old. When he'd finally been identified by his fingerprints, it turned out he was an eighteen-year old Guatemalan who had a work visa and had disappeared from an Oregon based tree planting crew.

Cove took another handful of water and dashed it onto the hot rocks. It hissed and spattered. The air in the tent was so hot he had to breathe slowly. His mind shifted to the sweats he'd done with his grandfather in his old lodge that had been made from brush and insulated with horse blankets.

An owl hooted up the creek, and he finally understood what his father had told him on the Cat's Ears.

His body was wet with flushed perspiration. He stayed in the tent for another twenty minutes and let his mind wander through the hills. When he crawled out, he laid down in the creek and let the water finish washing his body. After he'd cooled off, he got up and sat down on the table, listening to the warm night. Crickets called from the rocks across the creek. Moonlight was hitting the tops of the hills, but the face of the old man wasn't quite visible.

After fifteen minutes, his skin was dry. He heard a noise towards his house and saw a flashlight bouncing down the trail. He watched as the light grew closer. Annie was walking in front of the intruder and her tail was wagging.

"Hello, warden." The voice was sweet, feminine and filled with warmth. It came from Julie Lake. "Looks like you're having a camp out."

She put her arm around Cove's shoulder, kissed him on the cheek and moved to the fire. The flames illuminated her slim build and her bare legs. She was wearing shorts and a light V-necked top. The dancing flames caused her red hair to glow and move as if the wind were blowing.

She looked down at the empty bottle.

"I dumped it in the fire. It's gone." He took a deep breath. "I just took a sweat bath. It's like a sauna. Feels good."

She shined her light into the tent. "Would you mind if I took one?"

Cove used the shovel to pull the rocks out of the tent and replaced them with three more from the fire. Standing by the door, he said, "Crawl in and flick some water on the rocks."

She pulled him close and kissed his mouth. She smelled as fresh and warm as a summer rain. After a moment she pulled her top off, took him by the hand and pulled him into the tent. "I'm afraid of the dark."

A Note to the Reader

The idea for this story was hatched when I read a news article published in January, 2014. Two duck hunters had found a body northwest of Cody, Wyoming. The person's head had been cut off along with "unspecified body parts." The death was the result of multiple gunshot wounds. The victim was a Hispanic male who was wearing a piteado belt buckle. As I write this, the head and other body parts have not been found.

You may be wondering about my story angle of an illegal pesticide being used on a marijuana growing operation. A few years ago, I sat in on a briefing by California Fish and Wildlife concerning the environmental damages caused by illegal marijuana grows. (The body count associated with these operations includes deer, bears, birds and fish and the habitat damage is horrendous.) It is not unusual to find Temik, generically called aldicarb, being used at these California grows. In

Idaho, agents have found similar banned pesticides being used at outdoor grows. The labels on the containers are printed in Spanish.

The largest Idaho marijuana grow I am aware of was discovered south of Pocatello in 2012 and consisted of over 43,000 plants. The estimated value of the crop was eighty-million dollars. Bannock County sheriff, Lorin Nielson believed it was tied to a cartel. Evidence at the site indicated it had been in use for years.

I used to work with a game warden that was badly cut while checking anglers along the Boise River. When he approached a fisherman, the guy stepped toward him, took a swing and Dave blocked the blow with his forearm. The man took off running. Dave stopped his foot pursuit when he realized he'd been severely cut. The laceration went all the way to bone from his wrist to his elbow. Dave told me that for a long time he was afraid to go to sleep because when he did, he would have a horrifying dream of being beheaded. These are called night terrors, and they go far beyond nightmares. They are common with people suffering from post traumatic stress disorder. And so is alcohol abuse—so please don't take Charlie's dance with Jack Daniel's as a Native American issue. This is a story about an officer trying to continue his life while suffering from PTSD.

Morgan Creek is north of Challis. You can turn left onto the West Fork, take another left and drive to the head of Fourth Spring Creek. It's gorgeous country. There's a good view of the Cat's Ears from the top. I don't think you'll find the butte's name on a map but that's what it's called.

240

I hope this story stole you away. If you have a question about this book, or any of my others, please drop a note through my Facebook Author Page or my webpage at: www.tonylatham.net

Thanks!

-Tony H. Latham

CPSIA information can be obtained at www.ICGtesting.com
Printed in the USA
LVOW11s2133050616

491322LV00001BA/267/P